Merlin Built Stonehenge

Merlin Built Stonehenge

Bruce Bedlam

StonehengeLimited*publishers*
Registered Office
72 Callington Road
Saltash Cornwall PL12 6DY

Published in 2005
by StonehengeLimited*publishers*

Second Edition

Copyright © Bruce Bedlam 2005

ISBN 0 9549916 0 5

Cover illustration by Paul Burke
Printed by T J International

Foreword

Some readers may think that it is historically inconsistent to link the time of Stonehenge with that of Merlin. The great stone temple was built around 2000 BC, whereas the Arthurian Romances, in which Merlin plays a key role, are set in medieval times, so how can the latter have built the former?

There is an explanation! Stories of Arthur and Merlin were first recorded in Geoffrey of Monmouth's *Histories of the Kings of Britain* in 1138, and soon afterwards, on the orders of Henry II, re-told by a cleric called Wace in the form of a novel titled *Roman de Brut*. Wace even included in his manuscript an illuminated miniature showing Merlin directing the building of Stonehenge. These stories became very popular, especially in 12th Century France, where they were transformed into the Arthurian Romances by skilled storytellers, such as Marie de France, and the poet Chretien de Troyes.

These tales and romances have coloured our view of Arthur and Merlin to this day, so we tend to see them as medieval figures. Neither the French romancers, nor the historical chroniclers of Henry II's time, were the first to relate the deeds of Arthur and Merlin. In fact, the origins of these stories lie deep in Celtic Legend.

Acknowledgements

Thanks to John Pegg and HP.

A message in time

The word "Monument" comes from the word building and means "to remember". Buildings of high status were not built at random but in such a way that they could be rediscovered. Our ancestors knew that as long as the stones remained, the information would be carried and Stonehenge would last forever.

Dedicated to my four children
Eva, Hans, Hannah and Anja
and in Memory of Lars.

Prologue

They came under cover of darkness, twelve men dressed in leather. They looked like warriors but moved like shadows. It was the middle of the night and it was pouring with rain.

There was no obvious track but they knew the route; this was rough country with trees, shrubs and brambles everywhere. They did not intend to meet anyone this night; no one must know where they were going or what they were doing.

Their thoughts were on one objective; to deliver the chest they were carrying. It was strapped to a stretcher, a large box wrapped in sacking. Four men carried the stretcher; there was also a group leader and, ahead of him, a leading scout. Two men brought up the rear, listening and checking that they were not being followed. The other four were close to the stretcher, ready to take over the carrying at any time.

They had all sworn to give their lives to deliver the box, and nothing was going to get in their way. They knew that their task was vital; that they would rather die than fail to complete their mission.

Everything so far had gone to plan; they went over the last bound and they could see their final destination. It was a large round wooden hut with a thatched roof and double doors with no other apertures.

They stopped short and crouched in the shadows, waiting for a moment. Then the leader advanced towards the entrance and as he reached the doors they opened without a word being spoken. He then turned and gestured to his men, and they moved forward and without hesitation went straight inside.

Waiting for them in the middle of the room were two wooden trestles, illuminated by a single lamp. They placed the stretcher on the trestles and left the room immediately to take up positions outside, surrounding the hut like twelve pillars of strength. They stood there in the darkness and pouring rain, unflinching, with eyes like steel, guarding the master, obeying his instructions without question.

Inside the hut was a gathering of men and women, all obscured by the shadows; a lone man stepped forward into the light. He was wearing a long robe with a hood covering his head; only his hands could be seen as he started to undo the sacking. It was obvious that it had been he who had fastened it together by the way he pulled at the sacking and it fell away, to reveal a most beautiful casket.

This was made of wood with no carvings; it was purely functional and very well made. It was bound with strong cord, and someone had even taken the trouble to cut grooves for the cord to fit into. He knew which rope to pull and he quickly unfastened the tightly fitting twine.

There was absolute silence as the lid was slowly removed. Inside was something swaddled in fine linen, something valuable, priceless and awesome, but the existence of which no one must know. There had been years of preparation, but now the key to everything was here at last.

Chapter One

In an age long ago, a man named Whittle was preparing to set out on a journey. A messenger had come from Bracken, his tribal Chieftain, calling on him as his village's spokesman to attend an important meeting.

Such meetings were held to debate and discuss local affairs, and also to hear any messages or commands issued by the High Council, the country's governing body.

The place where meetings were held was many miles away, and Whittle had to make his way there on foot, horses being then rare and precious animals only used by the nobility. Tall and strong, Whittle was fortunately able to cover long distances with relative ease.

His village lay on the High Plain, just a short distance from the edge of an escarpment. Anyone standing between the trees beside the village and looking west could see right across the lowlands or levels. Much of the ground here was waterlogged as far as the eye could see, taking the form of a series of marshes and ponds interspersed with areas of higher ground. The latter were linked by a series of footpaths and strongly constructed wooden walkways.

Once in open countryside, Whittle would break into a steady, loping run that was not fast enough to tire him easily, but enabled him to cover the ground remarkably quickly.

Before leaving that morning his wife Jenny had prepared some food for him to eat on the journey, gutting a small piglet and plucking and dressing two quail which could be roasted on a makeshift spit when the time came. Along the way he would help himself to nuts, berries and fresh, ice-cold water from springs and rivers.

Summer was just reluctantly turning to autumn when the call came to Whittle. He would travel across miles and miles of open rolling countryside; there were no fences, walls or hedges to hinder his progress. Much of the land was also covered with forest, and well stocked with animals and birds; life, in fact, was bursting out of every wood and thicket. As Whittle strode along he was constantly seeing deer, rabbits, partridge, pheasant, ducks and all kinds of wildlife.

It was indeed a golden landscape, full of sunshine, birdsong and flowers. The promise of autumn abundance showed in the many apples, plums and blackberries; even acorns could be used for pig feed; there was certainly plenty of food at this time of year.

'Winter will be here soon,' murmured Whittle to himself, 'bringing more difficult times with it, but there's always food to be found for those who know where to look. People have worked out that the only way for us to survive is to work together and help each other.

'Neighbours are like brothers; all families are glad that there are others nearby when accidents or illnesses strike. That's why we've all come together to live in groups of huts which we call "villages".'

'I wonder how many there are,' he mused, 'we're told they're scattered all over the country, so there must be a lot. One thing I do know, the idea of families living close together makes good sense.'

Whittle was highly regarded by his neighbours, and had been a popular choice as village spokesman. People always knew where they stood with Whittle.

'By my deeds you shall know me' he used to say, and he had a reputation as a good, hard worker, honest and true to his word. He had a natural affinity with animals, and had spent his working life tending the village's herds of cattle and pigs, as well as the flocks of fowl, some of which had their wings clipped, others were kept in coops; they provided the villagers with both meat and eggs.

What others particularly liked about him was that he was not only a 'doer', but he was also a good listener, always ready to appreciate the advice of those who specialised in useful skills such as timber splitting, building huts, growing crops or hunting and trapping. Those who particularly impressed him were people who used their brains to puzzle things out, or were able to reason why certain things worked as they did, so that improvements could be made to make them more efficient when necessary. It was the thinkers, Whittle had found, who usually reaped the benefits of their ideas.

All this time, Whittle had been making his way automatically along the tracks towards the tribal meeting-place. When he stopped and looked about him he realised that he had come further than he thought, and that his legs, strong as they were, felt weary.

Deciding to rest for a while in the shade of an old sacred oak tree, which stood a short way ahead, he approached it with due reverence, bowing low before sitting down with his back against the trunk. Tree spirits were like old human folk, he thought, slow and kindly but capable of being roused to anger if they were not treated with due respect. There was an indefinable bond between men and trees; the forests were very ancient and the home of strange powers, yet the tree-spirits were prepared to sacrifice themselves to provide humankind with wood for shelter and many other uses.

Whittle felt comfortable with trees, 'But water-spirits living in rivers and streams,' he thought, 'are another matter entirely.' Capricious, moody and charming by turns, they could be very dangerous, luring men and women to drink or bathe and then either putting them under a spell or carrying them down through the water.

Anyone feeling thirsty and in need of a drink, as Whittle was now, needed to approach the little stream with great caution. He walked towards the bank slowly, saying the words he had been taught long ago by a wise woman, and then dropping into the open mouth of the spring an offering in the shape of a flint axe-head which he had been carrying in the big leather pouch at his belt. As it disappeared into the darkness of the small opening from where the spring emerged, Whittle could not repress a shudder at the thought of the many people who, all unsuspecting, had been taken there against their will.

He was glad of the warm setting sun on his back, and the reassuring evening light which it threw all around him, as he filled his wooden cup from the spring and returned thankfully to the shelter of the sacred tree. He quickly made a fire, roasted his piglet and enjoyed a satisfying, filling meal, following up with the nuts and fruits he had collected along the way, all washed down with the clear, cold spring water.

Then he carefully extinguished the fire, wrapped himself in his cloak and lay down under the tree to sleep, first surrounding himself with a circle of dry twigs which would alert him at once if any person or animal approached during the night.

Next morning he woke early, washed and ate again briefly, then set off again on the remainder of his journey. The path he took was one he had found many years ago, which took him on his way without passing any sign of human activity. Whittle liked to travel alone and keep his own counsel when going to a tribal meeting; it enabled him to marshal his thoughts and prepare the things he wanted to say there without any distractions along the way. As it was, he would arrive at the meeting early in the morning, refreshed and ready for a long day's discussions.

After a few more miles he saw smoke rising through the clear air in the distance and knew he would soon be approaching the meeting-place. When he arrived he found about twenty people already present, some busy cooking an appetising-smelling breakfast over the fires they had lit.

Whittle greeted the other village representatives as he met them; he already knew them all by name. The site had a relaxed, comfortable feel to it; there were no jealousies or bitter feuds among any of those present, whose numbers soon began to swell as more and more joined the gathering. There was an air of expectation as people were wondering what topics would be discussed this time, but while there were many waves and nods of greeting there was no deep conversation; no one wanted to pre-empt what would be said at the meeting.

Whittle knew he could always rely on his fellow-representatives to be as truthful and open as he would be himself, and he trusted the time-honoured process and methods by which they reached their decisions.

Apart from one or two minor village matters, he had nothing else to raise at the meeting. His main priority would be to listen well and absorb what he heard, so that when he returned to his village he would be able to give the others a clear, accurate account of the day's proceedings.

As soon as all those taking part had assembled, a horn was blown and everyone moved forward to take their places in the large round hut where, by tradition, the meeting was always held. They sat on wooden benches, placed in circles so that all present were facing into the middle of the room.

There was a hush, then into the centre strode the imposing, bearded figure of their tribal Chieftain. His name was Bracken, a tall, strong, broad-shouldered man who, in his day, had been a great warrior hero but was now coming up to fifty years of age. Although still far fitter than many younger men, age and the fact that he had held the Chieftainship for many years now had begun to take their toll, and the strain was starting to show.

Bracken had no interest in power for its own sake, but he did his duty and no one would have dreamed of challenging his authority. Everyone looked up to him; he was loved and revered by all, and made sure that every suggestion, problem or grievance raised and discussed would be personally referred by him to the High Council. At this particular meeting he had a matter of great importance to raise, but as he stood there, he showed no sign that anything special was afoot. Under Bracken's leadership everything was always dealt with calmly and in the correct order.

'Greetings!' he began, 'thanks to you all for coming, and welcome. The first thing I have to tell you is that two village representatives have been replaced since the last meeting, so we have two new members here today in their places. I will ask each in turn to stand up so that you can all see who they are. First is Gelp, from the village where the river joins; second is Mort, her village is at the edge of the bog swamp on this side of the level. I formally welcome them into this meeting on your behalf as representatives of their villages.

11

'Next, I am pleased to announce that there will be a festival held on the upland field, on the next full moon. I have appointed Mohen to take charge and organise the proceedings, and to answer all your questions. Will you please stand, Mohen, so all can recognise and remember you? Thank you!'

A large, capable-looking woman, Mohen was already known to many and popular for her efficient organisation which had helped to make other festivals a success, so she rose to a round of applause, smiling broadly and waving in acknowledgement before resuming her seat.

After these introductions the meeting was thrown open to all, with every man and woman having the opportunity to speak on behalf of his or her village, voicing news, problems and suggestions which were discussed at length. Some of the decisions they came to were voted on and approved by the majority by means of a show of hands. Major decisions would then be taken by Bracken to the High Council for further discussions.

It took several hours to debate all the topics raised, after which Bracken announced there would be a short adjournment before he raised a particularly important subject. Glad of a break, those present filed out to avail themselves of the ample supplies of food and drink that had been prepared earlier.

After sufficient time had passed the horn sounded again and the village representatives returned to their places, wondering what this important matter of which Bracken had spoken might be.

When they were all seated Bracken returned, and stood in the centre as before. This time he was carrying the tribal Stone of Office, his symbol of authority presented to him personally by the King when he was elected tribal Chieftain many years ago. It was a large black stone, cut and tooled into a thick ring. Many years ago it had been placed over the trunk of a specially selected sapling, and when this had grown sufficiently to fill out the space within the ring and hold it firmly in place, the tree was cut down, prepared to the right length and carved into a staff.

Everyone knew that the appearance of this meant something very special was afoot, and they listened eagerly as Bracken began to speak.

'Once again,' he began, 'I have important things to say to you. There will be changes coming in the next few years that will affect us all. They will concern not just our tribe, but everyone throughout the land. I have been informed of this by the High Council; we must all make ready for the biggest undertaking that our people have ever achieved. What exactly it is, we do not yet know, but we must be

13

prepared to take part in a great project which will last for a period of years.

'Given the length of time involved, and the fact that I, your Chieftain, am not getting any younger, I feel it would be unwise for you to have a change in leadership during such a critical period. I therefore recommend that a new Chieftain be chosen!'

There was an immediate reaction to this startling turn of events, and people began talking excitedly to each other about it.

Bracken held up his Stone of Office for silence, and within seconds everyone fell quiet.

'We have until the festival to choose and elect the new Chieftain,' he said firmly, 'no mistakes must be made, and he – or she – will be named at the festival in front of the whole tribe!'

After this startling revelation the meeting broke up swiftly; most people, Whittle among them, were eager to get back to their villages and spread the news as quickly and as widely as possible.

Whittle returned along the same tracks he had so recently followed, but more swiftly this time as he had so much to tell. When he reached home, his wife Jenny was nowhere to be seen, but his little girl Rosy, fair-haired like her mother and bright-eyed, came running to greet him overjoyed to see him again.

Whittle picked her up in his arms, smiled at her and asked 'Where is your mother and the others?'

'Down at the bottom there, collecting herbs,' she answered eagerly, jabbing the air with a podgy finger, 'someone in the village is sick, and Mummy has gone with old Ruen to help her look for a doctor plant.'

Tired after all his travelling, Whittle decided that they could come and find him, so he sat down on a wooden bench outside his main door and relaxed in the sunshine while he waited for them to return.

First to arrive was his son Boy. A tall fifteen-year-old, the lad was dark-haired and good-looking, spirited and sturdily built like Whittle himself. Somehow he had grown up without a name, and was always just known as 'Boy'; maybe, thought Whittle, he will choose one himself one day and surprise us all.

'Well, Boy' he said out loud in greeting, 'is everything to your liking?'

Boy smiled and, without answering, sat down next to his father in silence. It was the same when Jenny and the others returned. They knew that Whittle would say nothing more until the entire village was present.

News of his return spread rapidly, and with it the idea that he had brought important tidings. More and more began to gather around him, until soon everyone was waiting expectantly for him to begin.

First of all, he related how the King and his ministers were planning a very big change that would involve everyone in the country, and would continue for several years. This was exciting, but a bit much for ordinary folk to take in, particularly as it was still in the future and Whittle could not say what exactly was involved. The news about Bracken, however, was something everybody could understand, and indeed many present were too young to remember what life was like before he took office. The choosing of a new Chieftain would be a very big occasion, one of the most important moments in their lives.

Once the news had sunk in, people began eagerly discussing who might be chosen as the new Chieftain, and the expectation and excitement leading up to the festival grew as the weeks went by. Everyone was relieved when the time of the full moon finally arrived.

On the morning of the festival, all those capable of carrying items to the sacred site did so. Food and drink were the main items, along with cups, plates and tables on which to place them, together with wooden benches for those wanting to rest. Additionally, warm cloaks and blankets were also taken for use if required. Everyone lent a hand, even the village's oldest inhabitant, Old Moff, who was so frail he slowed everyone down to such an extent that it would have been easier to carry him, but he insisted on bringing things and making his own way unaided.

People from other villages were also arriving at the sacred site, bringing their own contributions to the festival. Boy was in his element; he was so excited that he would run up along the line and back again time after time, not wanting to miss a thing. So many people were on the move that everything was happening at once; people were chatting, laughing and calling to each other while the little children were running about under everybody's feet.

All present were enjoying themselves including Whittle himself, who was happy feeling the pleasure and wonder of such an occasion. This was a spiritual time, when feelings were heightened by the sheer volume of people. The closer Whittle and his family got to the festival field the more people came into view, until they finally arrived to find themselves in the middle of a great throng. There were hundreds of people, all mingling together and happy to see each other.

Overlooking the crowd which filled the field was a large platform on which they could see Mohen, with Bracken standing beside her. As she raised her arms a sudden silence fell across the gathering, apart from a few babies crying.

Bracken opened the proceedings by calling out 'Welcome to you all! Before we start the celebrations, let us remember who we are and what the Gods have made us. We give thanks to them on this day, as we celebrate with our families and friends. We rejoice in the fact that we are alive and present here today.'

Mohen then gestured at a man stationed at the top of a tall tower beside the platform; he immediately responded by blowing the Tribal Horn to proclaim the festival open. Drums began to beat, and the people started to clap and sing with the rhythm. There was dancing and merrymaking, with everyone having a wonderful time. In the midst of this, three weddings were celebrated and eight new babies were announced.

Everyone knew that the finale of the whole festival would be the naming of their new Chieftain, so they were waiting expectantly when at exactly noon on the second day the Horn was blown again and a procession of all the villages' leaders began. They walked right around the outside of the main crowd and finished in front of the platform. From this vantage-point, Bracken addressed the whole tribe.

'The day has arrived,' he announced, 'when we proclaim a new Chieftain, a man or woman who will speak on our behalf to the High Council. Someone who will help us make decisions and lead us into the new era we are promised. There have been many meetings and discussions, and our wise men have finally agreed. There is one who has been chosen above all others. He is a man of great honour, wisdom and strength, but above all else he is a man of humility and spirituality. His name is – Whittle!'

Whittle was utterly dumbfounded! He could not believe he had heard his name announced; how could they have come to such a decision? But now everyone was cheering, and Whittle was hoisted onto the platform by many willing hands. Here, Bracken assured him he would still be on hand to give him help and advice whenever he needed it.

'All will be well!' he cried triumphantly.

Still overwhelmed by the suddenness of it all, Whittle bowed and waved to the cheering sea of faces below him, then was led away by Bracken to a quiet place where they could talk undisturbed.

Later that afternoon he was led onto the platform again, this time holding the imposing Stone of Office as proof of his new authority. As he raised it high in the air, there was a mighty roar of approval. The new Chieftain was accepted by all.

But this was only the first of many great events that would affect the tribe as, unknown to them, momentous changes were taking place all over the country.

Chapter Two

The King awoke.

Day would not dawn for many hours, but a bright beam of moonlight shone through the tall window-opening in the high-ceilinged chamber where he had enjoyed a short but restful sleep. The large bed on which he lay had proved comfortable, and he had been protected from the chill night air by a covering of warm furs.

It had been dark when he retired the night before by candlelight, and he had paid little attention to his surroundings. Now he looked around him curiously, and was relieved to see that his travelling cases and boxes were piled neatly in a corner; his gold crown lay on the table, together with his precious gem-studded gold chains, rings and other jewellery. His fine robes and other garments had been hung up carefully by his personal servant, named Crelin, who was still asleep on the floor, lying as he always did across the doorway to protect his royal master from any intruders.

Despite being in strange surroundings, the King had no fear of anything untoward occurring. He knew that his host, King Godfrey, had appointed his champion Galeron to take charge of security. He had posted guards outside in the hallway, and the building was well secured.

His Majesty King Godfrey had need to look to his security, because the compound was presently holding within its walls not only the King of the Isle of Breton, but Kings, Queens, Emperors and other royal personages from all over the known world. It was the largest gathering of rulers that had ever taken place; they had all come together in alliance for a week to discuss matters of mutual interest, including trade, foreign affairs and an exchange of ideas, particularly innovations from different countries which might be of benefit to others.

To assist him at these discussions the King had, like his fellow rulers, brought with him his most trusted Ministers, advisers and interpreters, as well as a train of guards, attendants and servants; in all, he headed a delegation of some thirty loyal subjects.

This was his first overseas visit for many years; he had crossed the water to meet with his friends and to observe the different peoples whose culture was strange to him, all in the interest of good relations between all countries attending.

Carnac was chosen as the right place to hold this vast gathering, because the site was of great antiquity and venerated as such. It contained over 3,000 stone monuments, multi-stone dolmens and single menhirs or standing stones, hewn from the local granite. The original carvers of these massive menhirs, many weighing hundreds of tons, had laid them out in straight lines in long avenues stretching for miles, all in alignment with the sun. Everyone who came to the area was amazed at the strength, determination and ingenuity of the people who had constructed such a complex; the atmosphere of mystery and power surrounding it made this the perfect site to celebrate the official opening of the rulers' week-long deliberations.

Ancient ritual, however, laid down that all ceremonies marking the beginning of great events must have everyone involved gathered together to be present at sunrise. The King knew that he had been wakened by the sound of stirring elsewhere in the fortress, and that he too must prepare to attend the ceremony and give thanks for the dawn on such a special day.

As he rose, Crelin leaped up, fully awake in an instant, and began to help his royal master prepare. After holding the towel ready for his ablutions, Crelin began by setting out the King's tunic and heavy royal robes before helping him to dress. After the robes came the brooches, neck-chains, rings and other gem-studded gold jewellery, the richness of which denoted the King's royal status and his seniority within the hierarchy of rulers now gathered together.

The King smiled to himself as Crelin fussed around him, making sure that his robes fell in their correct folds, straightening a brooch here and a chain there before carefully picking up the magnificently jewelled and ornamented crown and placing it reverently on the royal head.

'That will do, Crelin,' he murmured, 'if I'm not ready now I never will be!'

Crelin could not resist giving one more tweak to the long, fur-trimmed train before calling the King's personal guards to bring torches in order to light the way for His Majesty to proceed to the Royal Enclosure.

As he walked along, flanked by his escort, the King was preparing himself for one of the greatest moments in history, when the three greatest rulers of what is now Northern Europe would meet together for the first time. He was the King of the Isle of Breton; King Godfrey was ruler of the central mainland or interland; and King Holger of Dansk was monarch of all the northern territories. They had held each other in the highest respect for many years; now this was an opportunity to forge that friendship into a link that would last a lifetime.

Once outside, he found other monarchs also proceeding to the site. It was a spectacular sight with bright, flaring torches moving through the night and making the moon's light pale by comparison.

The Royal Enclosure had special stands covered with a temporary thatched roof. In the middle were three huge seats for the Three Kings, who would sit together. Additionally there were raised tiers of wooden seating to give all the other royal visitors a good view of the proceedings. The Royal Enclosure had been sited so that they could look straight down the impressive line of huge menhirs, which would leap into prominence when they were bathed in the first rays of the morning sun.

All the rulers were led to their places by deferential attendants and seated in strict accordance with protocol. The King took his place; he bowed and gestured to his fellow dignitaries but there was no formal acknowledgement at this time as all were focused on the event in hand. Galeron had planned the ceremony with meticulous care, so the royal spectators did not have long to wait before it commenced.

First there was a faint glow in the eastern sky, which grew larger and brighter with surprising speed until suddenly the appearance of the top of the sun's golden disc sent a ray of light directly down on the row of standing stones. Another day had dawned, the sun had returned, and life was renewed once more.

Suddenly, at the precise moment of the sun's first appearance, a low rumbling became audible in the distance. As it got nearer it became louder and those present, realised with a thrill that it was the sound of thousands of drums. All were beating out their message of joy at the new dawn in a wonderful rhythm with different tones and beats which were all merging together in a triumphant salute to the magnificent Sun God.

While the drums continued to sound, great crowds of people slowly came into view at the far end of the long line of stones. They proceeded to advance between the stones towards the Royal Enclosure; as they came nearer, more and more spectators began filling up the space beneath where the royal visitors were also watching.

From where he sat, high in the stand as befitted his seniority, the King could look over their heads at the advancing throng, all dressed in multi-coloured ceremonial robes and many carrying elaborately embroidered and painted banners, or flying the flags of their respective tribes. It was a truly spectacular sight.

For an instant all was quiet, and then equally suddenly everyone on the ground broke out in a joyous response to a bright new day and in greeting to their very important visitors. People, some with ladders, helped others climb on top of the stones. Those who had done so waved their banners and flags; others blew whistles and horns, whereupon the drums took up their exciting rhythm again and everyone cheered.

The assembled royals waved their thanks and appreciation to the crowds, which prompted even louder cheering. Then, rising to their feet and leaving the stand, all the monarchs were ushered into a long procession that slowly moved past either side of the Royal Enclosure.

Looking at the vast ranks of spectators, the King was glad to see that they were all in a festive mood, glad and happy to share in this wonderful and unique occasion. They reflected a feeling of joyful optimism that all was right with the world at this time.

The crowds studied the royal procession with great interest, and much admired the King. He stood out because of his height and particularly regal bearing, looking very grand in his fine robes and magnificent gold crown, with its many-coloured jewels flashing and glittering as they were touched by the bright morning sunlight. To those who knew about such things, his country, the Isle of Breton, was held in the highest esteem. As King, he represented his people with honour, pride and majesty and was given the greatest respect accordingly at this royal pageant. It was an occasion he would never forget, seeing so many of his fellow monarchs from different nations, all meeting together in one accord with a common purpose: the betterment of mankind.

As he walked slowly along, he found himself near his old friend King Holger, ruler of the Dansk. Holger was a rugged, powerfully built man, with such an imposing, regal presence that he seemed larger than life. A famous warrior champion in his youth, he still looked the part in later middle age, despite his long plaited hair and beard. His robes of state were based on his soldier's uniform, except now, his breastplate was solid silver and his short cloak was made of velvet, the hem sewn with precious stones.

The King greeted him warmly, calling out 'Hail, Holger! It is good that we meet again in this place.'

'It is good to be here at such a time,' the ruler of Dansk replied; 'there is much to be done for our people.'

'King Godfrey deserves praise for hosting so great an event; his people certainly are fortunate indeed.'

'Could your country surpass what has been established here?' enquired Holger.

'I have no doubt we could,' smiled the King, 'my people are renowned for their intellect and, who knows, we might surprise you all one day!'

They laughed together as they walked along, two of the most important and powerful men alive. They stopped and waited for their host, King Godfrey, who was smiling and waving to the crowd.

After greeting his many guests, he finally turned and approached his friends. Some seven years younger than the other two monarchs, he was an equally tall, strong and imposing figure. Like the King of Breton, he was well-groomed and good-looking, with brown eyes and shoulder-length hair of a matching colour, while his ready smile revealed perfectly even, gleaming white teeth. He wore a large-calf-length brown fur coat, which would blow open in the wind from time to time to reveal that under it he was wearing a large, broad leather belt studded with rubies, emeralds, diamonds and other large gems.

They looked at each other, a big grin broke out on each of their faces and they all began to laugh. King Godfrey gripped the two of them and held them in a warm embrace.

'Well, we meet at last, it is so good to see you both again. We have much to talk about; come, let us proceed together.'

They went to where his Champion, Galeron, had marshalled together their respective attendants, who were waiting with three magnificent horses. Even though they only had a relatively short distance to cover, to be riding such rare and costly animals in the procession added to the air of majesty and grandeur which befitted such an important occasion.

From the Royal Enclosure, the procession wound its way to the Great Hall. This magnificent structure was constructed especially for the occasion and was huge, made visually even bigger by its total lack of any internal supports. The sense of importance it projected, and the awe with which it was regarded, made it truly unique.

It was over a hundred and twenty feet long, and the roof span measured no less than forty feet across the beam; this was known as the Henge or Hang of the roof, a word which was to echo down the centuries in the name 'Hangar'.

This was King Godfrey's masterpiece; all the monarchs who entered the vast space were instantly aware of the monumental grandeur of the place. They were the highest dignitaries in the known world, and this was the ultimate gesture, designed to give them the due respect and honour befitting their status.

Inside, Galeron, as head of security and master of ceremonies, had prepared the Great Hall for a special day of celebration, to follow the Ceremony of the Sunrise. He stood just inside the great doors to welcome his sovereign's guests; an imposing figure, similar in age and height to his master and friend. He had been a great fighter in his youth, although his hair was now greying, and he was known and respected throughout the land as a national hero.

As a reminder of his military past, he usually wore a bronze shoulder plate, except on great occasions of state like the present, when he exchanged it for a full mantlet made of solid gold, which fitted across his shoulders under a richly coloured cape. As master of ceremonies, he ensured that everything which took place in the Great Hall went with parade-ground precision.

On this day, and throughout the following week, he had arranged that all the royal guests would be provided with ample fare, both before and after all the discussions and exchanges of information took place. Long tables had been set out and laden with a bewildering array of food and drink, to provide a banquet lavish enough to satisfy the appetites of all those present.

Nor were their other senses forgotten; at the end of each day the feasting would be enlivened by a series of spectacular entertainments, including jugglers, acrobats, fire-eaters, knife-throwers and the most delectable dancing girls, all accompanied by large numbers of skilled musicians, playing on instruments of many different kinds.

During that preparatory week, much new thinking had been aired, and many old acquaintances re-forged. And when the festivities finally got underway, it was with a sense of achievement and of duty well done that the royal delegates assembled once more, to enter the Great Hall, where they could relax and enjoy each others' company. The King, Holger and Godfrey sat next to each other, talking about old times. King Godfrey ate and drank sparingly, but Holger's appetite was remarkable; he could wolf down a chicken in about three mouthfuls, and drain his cup in one draft, the mead seemingly having no ill effects.

'He obviously takes all his pleasures in the same spirit,' said King Godfrey, as Holger cheerfully bellowed his enthusiasm for a particularly sinuous group of dancing girls.

One of the highlights of this first evening had been arranged by one of the guests; it was a complete surprise for everyone. A horn was blown for silence, and then eight strong men carried a large cage into the centre of the Great Hall. Nobody could see what it contained, as a heavy black cloth was draped over it. The assembled company stared at it with growing interest, wondering what would happen next.

Then suddenly, making everyone jump, an angry deep low rumbling growl came from beneath the cloth, a growl of such sustained ferocity that it made the hair at the back of people's necks stand on end. Then several attendants whisked the cloth away, revealing the most powerful beast that anyone present had ever seen.

It was the stuff of nightmares; huge, covered with black matted hair out of which gleamed wide yellow eyes ablaze with vicious fury, together with the biggest, evilly gleaming teeth and claws capable of ripping prey to shreds in seconds. At first it cowered from the light, then hurled itself against the bars of its cage and let out roar after roar of fury. It was a creature of sheer power, born to kill; a terrifying spectacle.

One or two guests were brave or foolhardy enough to go and inspect it, getting close as if daring it to strike at them.

This roused it to even greater fury; the beast's instincts of anger and hunger caused it to roar at ever-increasing volume, and, stretching an enormous paw suddenly through the bars, it caught one man's cloak and ripped it from his shoulders. After that, it was swiftly removed, leaving the

Great Hall buzzing with excitement. Even though many, like the King, thought it a somewhat crude way to impress one's guests, nevertheless it was spectacular.

During the remainder of the week, while somewhat more restrained banquets were held every evening, daytimes saw the assembled monarchs and their advisers kept busy with many planned meetings and group discussions on ideas for improvement.

When all the events were over, the King had one last visitor; for once it was not a fellow monarch. His Chief Minister had advised him to see a traveller who had come from far away. The man gave no name or title, or even his country of origin, and yet he had the power to persuade his very experienced royal counsellor to recommend that the King grant him an audience.

This was indeed strange, thought the King, and he was curious to see what manner of person the foreign stranger might be. They met, just the two of them with no attendants or guards present, in the Audience Chamber of the King's royal suite. The King was already seated when the stranger entered, bowed low without speaking and then stood respectfully before him. Eager to examine him, the King gestured to another chair that had been placed opposite; bowing once more, the man silently took his seat.

The traveller was wearing a close-fitting type of hood, embroidered with small gems, and he wore long robes that shimmered with gold and silver threads. This man was different, his face was clean and smooth, his gestures were graceful and yet he was astute, alert and very intelligent; possibly, thought the King, he was a scribe or a scholar. He gestured to the man to explain himself; with a nod of his head, the stranger began to speak.

'It is a great honour to meet you, your Majesty,' he began, 'your country has a reputation for being one of the most civilised in the known world.' As the King silently acknowledged the greeting, but did not reply, he continued: 'I would like to visit your country, with your Majesty's permission.'

The King was growing ever more curious as to who this man was, but felt he should not compromise his royal dignity by making his curiosity appear too obvious, answering only: 'You may speak to one of my Ministers and perhaps a visit could be arranged.'

'Thank you, Lord King,' came the reply, 'I hope that one day I can be of service to you and your country. Meanwhile, I bring you a gift, which I trust you will accept.'

So saying, he took a leather pouch from his belt and, opening it up, produced a gleaming, transparent sphere with an intricately carved wooden stand, and placed it on the table between them.

The King looked at it in amazement and fascination; glass was unknown to him, and in his eyes the object before him appeared like a large, shining ball of water. He reached out cautiously to touch it with one finger, then drew his hand swiftly back. To his amazement, the globe which looked so delicate and frail was in fact solid! Before he could ask even one of the questions which crowded into his mind, the stranger spoke again, saying:

'May good fortune continue to bless your Majesty.'

Then he was gone, with not another word. 'Who was he?' the King wondered.

He was left to muse on this strange encounter; it was one he knew he would never forget. Looking intently into the shining crystal ball, still on the table where the stranger had left it, he reflected on their meeting, just as his face was reflected in its shining surface. The man was obviously foreign, yet appeared completely at home in what to him were strange surroundings and spoke with great ease and authority.

How had this meeting come to pass? The King knew nothing about him, yet felt certain the stranger posed no threat; on the contrary, he found himself hoping that they would meet again soon. He was indeed greatly pleased as he sat and continued to marvel at the strange and beautiful gift he had so unexpectedly received.

Chapter Three

'Father?' Boy's voice suddenly broke the hushed silence of a late, golden autumn evening. He and Whittle were sitting on a wooden bench outside the family hut, relaxing at the end of a hard day and watching the light slowly fade to a soft twilight.

Whittle was startled out of his reverie, glad to hear the questioning note in his son's voice. He was proud of his son's curiosity and the way he questioned things, pleased that he had inherited the ability to be a good listener. Sometimes a particular answer would spark another question from him; during the day they had been talking about Whittle's new role as Chieftain and they would indulge in a regular debate about some method of procedure or how to conduct one's self at a meeting. Boy was quick to understand even quite complex subjects with a keen intelligence that Whittle felt would take his son far as he grew older.

Then Boy repeated 'Father?' a bit louder, and Whittle realised that in following his train of thought he had failed to respond.

'Well, Boy, what's on your mind?' he asked, wondering what the question might be this time.

'I heard in the village that the King has gone overseas. Does that mean when you go to represent us at the meeting, the Chieftains will rule the country?'

'No, it certainly doesn't. No one can ever take the place of the King! Let me explain how these things are organised; it will be useful for you to know in the future.'

'Thank you, Father,' Boy murmured quietly, always glad to add to his stock of knowledge.

Whittle continued: 'We are a very small part of what they call the great order of society that helps to run this country.' The very smallest unit is this village – there are many hundreds, just like ours, scattered all over the land. Each one has a representative, who goes when summoned to attend gatherings in each region. All the representatives are under the authority of a powerful tribal Chieftain, like me, who presides over all the debates and discussions. After several days, when we've come to our conclusions and decisions, it is the Chieftain's responsibility to carry these to important meetings of the High Council.

'This is the way the will of the people is channelled forward to be heard and acted upon. At the very heart of the country lies the biggest settlement of all; this is where the governing body called the High Council is based. Decisions made here are then passed on to a group of wise men known as 'Elders' for approval. They represent and act for the King, who is our absolute ruler; everything is carried out in his name and with his authority – subject, of course, to the blessing of the High Priest, who ensures that nothing is done which might offend the Gods.'

'What happens then, when the King is away from the country? He can't rule here whilst he is there, surely?'

Whittle smiled inwardly; Boy was very quick to spot a flaw in what he was being told, and queried it accordingly.

'While he is away', Whittle agreed, 'in his absence, all his affairs are dealt with by his Ministers of the Royal Court, who work closely with the Elders so that they all make the right decisions when debating law, solving disputes and authorising requests made by the Chieftains and the High Council.'

'But didn't you say the High Council does all that?' interjected Boy, 'surely those wise men don't just do the same things as each other? It would be such a waste of their time!'

'No,' Whittle replied, 'the High Council listen to all the local matters and the Chieftains' views which are brought from all over the country, and there may be information from abroad to take into consideration; again, all these things will affect their decisions. The High Council examine all the evidence and decide which items should be submitted to the Elders for eventual royal approval.'

'Just how big is this great settlement?' said Boy, 'how many people live there?'

'It's a really large, thriving community', began Whittle, 'with, oh, there must be 30,000 people or more spread out in a large area. The population is much closer together, the nearer you get to the centre. We, for example, live on the outer edge of this vast settlement. The further away you live, the less populated it will be, although there are some other great settlements to the far North, but nothing like as big as this one.

'Remember all the men and women who make up the High Council live here, together with their families, as well as the ordinary people. It is a rich place, with a better standard of living than anywhere else in the land. Peaceful too, where everyone manages to live and work together in harmony, making it a good, secure environment for bringing up children. When you're older, you'll travel there and see it for yourself. There's an atmosphere of long standing stability with everyone believing in and trusting the system, which has led to the growth of a quality of life that is remarkable in this or I should imagine any other age.'

'How did the people manage to get this "quality of life"?' Boy found it difficult to grasp quite what something called quality of life actually was, but was determined that he would find out.

'It was brought about by all the people working together,' Whittle explained. 'Their leaders set an example by being good, honest men and women who were true to their word, able to face the facts, and prepared to stand up for their beliefs. In this way they earned the respect of the people, who followed their advice, pooled their resources, and were able to develop a wide variety of different skills as a result of their mutual co-operation. This helped them to become well off by trading goods among themselves as well as other parts of the country and even abroad. The specialist skills, used to benefit all, soon included farming, weaving, potting, crop growing, breeders and herdsmen and many more. The resources of each individual person were pooled to help the community grow and flourish.'

'But if they were always producing the same things,' Boy remarked thoughtfully, 'wouldn't they have become just stick-in-the-muds, never doing anything different?'

'Ah,' Whittle replied, 'but that's just what they didn't do. Things didn't stand still. People were able to specialise, so they were able to give more attention to their craft or trade and so could think up better and more efficient ways of doing things.

'Growers of corn, for example, came to realise that scattering the seed on the land was rather inefficient, so they developed a way of cutting grooves in the land into which the seed could be sown. This new method made sure it didn't blow away, and allowed it to get more nourishment from the earth; the result was healthier crops that gave a bigger yield.'

'That's true!' Boy chipped in, 'I've heard the village farmers saying they've never known such harvests as we get nowadays.'

'Quite right,' nodded Whittle, 'and it's not just the farmers who are seeing better times. Take the bakers; they've learned how to build bigger and better ovens so they can bake more and tastier loaves, so that in turn, we're all better fed.'

Whittle went on, 'There has been a huge development in objects of trade. Those who specialise in how to produce gold and silver have found better ways to make the finest trinkets and jewellery in greater quantities that would please the most noble of men and women.

'So,' Whittle continued, 'to use a couple of important words, what with the "politics" of a system that represents everyone and is fair to all, and the "economics" of buying, selling and trading in a way that makes people better off, it's no wonder that the biggest, most central settlement is also the centre of power. From this central hub of our civilisation, controls reach out like a great web, binding the whole country in a long-standing and efficient social structure which has been steadily improved down the generations.'

'Why was this particular part of the country chosen as the place for such an important settlement?' asked Boy.

'There are many answers to that,' responded Whittle thoughtfully, 'and they go back many thousands of years. I'm not learned in the wisdom of the past like some, and I know nothing about sacred rituals or calculations, but what I do know is that it has always been considered to be the centre of all things. That is why the King's royal court and the various governing bodies are all based there. The High Council, for instance, meet in their large circular wooden buildings and there are the biggest earthworks of all time, these are great enclosures for the Chieftains to gather in.'

'That includes you too now, Father!' Boy added proudly.

Whittle smiled wryly, murmuring something about high office but a heavy burden none the less, and now, finding it hard to follow Bracken, who had done so well over the years.

'Of course,' he pointed out, 'there are many different types of Chieftain, greater and lesser in rank, status, age and experience. Yet, varied as we, are the system ensures that no one Chieftain can gain too much power and become stronger than any of the others. True, some of the senior ones are known as High Chieftains and wear special badges of rank (Gold Spangles) denoting their level of honour, while other Chieftains carry staffs or maces. For my part, I will carry the tribal Stone of Office; from this, others will see my level of importance and where I will be placed at the meetings.'

'Who looks after and organises all the meetings of the Chieftains and the High Council, then?' queried Boy. 'They must be kept pretty busy with all the comings and goings.'

'There is one man in charge; his name is Brenon,' Whittle told him. 'He is responsible for keeping order at the meetings, and everyone looks to him because he decides in what sequence debates will take place. He decides who will speak, and for how long. He oversees all the proceedings, and is the ultimate authority who rules on the way things are done, which they call "protocol".'

'I can see how all these people are subject to the King, whatever their titles,' said Boy, 'but earlier you said that the High Priest also had to be present to ensure that nothing was said or done to offend the Gods. Who is more powerful, then, the King or the Gods?'

'No human being, from the humblest villager to the King himself in all his majesty, is more powerful than the Gods!' replied Whittle, somewhat taken aback by this. 'The King rules the country and its people, but the Gods rule everything – the sky, the sun, the moon, the stars, the storms, the rain, the wind and all living creatures; that means everyone, including the King. That's why the High Priest is so important, and why our ceremonies, festivals and rituals are so central to our lives. At your age, you may only see the dancing and the merrymaking, but there's much more to it than that – which again you will find out as you get older. There are dates and times of the year which are marked and respected. There is time to celebrate when the harvest is safely gathered in. We stand in awe and wait for the morning sun to rise on the longest day. That's why the sacred sites are so important, why all the priests and other wise men gather there in one place. This one place is more sacred than any other; it is the hub of all things, what I have heard the priests call the "axis of creation". It is where everything comes together and connects – the Solstices, the Equinoxes and time itself. These are deep things we are touching on; I haven't all the answers but believe me, it does not get more powerful than this, for the Gods are all-powerful in this life and the next.'

'Has the site been important for a very long time, then?' queried Boy.

'Oh, since before time began, I should think,' Whittle replied, uncertain how to explain in simple terms something he did not fully understand himself. 'The same rituals have taken place for hundreds – the priests say possibly thousands – of years. Its origins are lost in time, and no one knows how it was discovered, so long ago. In the centre of this mysterious place is a group of stones, and tradition has it that they hold within them a very strong and ancient power carrying great authority.'

'What else is there to see besides the stones, then,' said Boy, 'and do people go there to worship the Gods?'

'All you will see when you go there is a large circle cut in the earth, about three hundred feet across, with the sacred stones in the centre. So holy is the ground inside the circle that no one other than priests are allowed to enter. I have heard it called "the place closest to the Gods", and somehow the stones channel and reflect something of their

47

power, with an energy flow no living being can understand. The King himself is given the power to rule by the Gods, and he is the only person allowed to touch the stones. He is the King chosen by the Gods and no one can question his authority.'

Boy was silent, trying to remember and absorb all that he had been told, and was quiet and withdrawn for the remainder of the evening. That night he lay awake and thought about the King, what it would be like to be close to the Gods. Then he felt a strange feeling running through his body, a deep sense of knowing that all would be well; with this, his eyes closed and he was soon fast asleep.

Chapter Four

Following his father's explanation of how the King ruled the country with his Elders and High Council, Boy dreamed of great gatherings of Chieftains who had pride and nobility, where men and women talked with honour and dignity; they were the ones who would decide what the future would bring. His imagination was running in all directions, until he made up his mind somehow to go and see the Royal Palace for himself.

When Boy asked Whittle to take him there, his father dismissed it as a childish fancy. But when after a couple of weeks Boy was as determined as ever to see where the King lived, he agreed that they would make the journey together. Because Whittle's post as Chieftain involved him regularly being away from the village, he had no trouble in arranging for one of his neighbours to look after his animals during his absence so, much to Boy's delight, they were able to set out in just a few days' time. As an added surprise for Boy, Whittle had arranged the journey so that they would arrive at the Royal Palace on the very day the King would be returning home from his foreign visit.

When they neared the middle of the great settlement, Boy became more and more aware of the ever-increasing

49

number of huts and buildings that crowded together on every side. Then suddenly he stopped dead and just stood speechless with amazement and wonder, as immediately ahead of him rose what seemed like a gigantic mountain crowned with huge wooden walls which had towers and turrets.

'Wh... whatever is th... that?' he managed to gasp out to Whittle. 'Do giants live there?'

Whittle explained that Boy was in fact looking at the actual Royal Palace he had been so determined to come and see.

'The Royal Court of King Arthur,' he went on, 'was built on the largest man-made mound in the world. It took countless teams of workers years to move millions of tons of earth and heap them up in a series of huge ramparts to create a vast, table-topped mountain. This has served as a secure, well-protected and fortified base on which to erect the Royal Palace itself and all the buildings surrounding it.'

'From here,' said Boy, 'it has the look of a grim and forbidding fortress.'

'Very true,' nodded Whittle, 'and any foolish enough to attack it would suffer certain defeat. But inside, protected by those strong defences, the King and Queen, the Royal family and the whole Court make up a beautiful community which lives peacefully and happily in carefully-planned buildings which radiate out from the Royal apartments in a series of large rooms linked by halls, passages and corridors leading to open areas.'

'It must be wonderful up there,' sighed Boy. 'Have you ever seen the King, Father?'

'Not close to,' admitted Whittle, 'but I have been in the crowds cheering him many times as he rode by in procession.'

'Talking of crowds,' said Boy, 'there seem to be an awful lot of people going towards the Palace like us.'

Whittle smiled to himself; 'Yes,' he said, 'it just so happens that today the King comes back from his foreign visit, and they all want to greet him on his return.'

'Oh, Father!' Boy was overjoyed. 'You mean you planned this so we could see him!' He was almost dancing with excitement as they got nearer and nearer to the foot of the great mound, swept along in a great throng of happy and excited people.

Whittle decided to position himself beside a grassy bank, and hoisted his son up onto the top so he would have a good view. After scanning the approach road and seeing nothing yet, Boy turned and gazed up at the Palace ramparts, craning his neck back to see if he could make anything out so high above him.

Suddenly he cried out, 'Oh, look, Father, there's someone peering down at us!' Although Whittle's sight was good, it was not as keen as Boy's, and he could not make anyone out.

But Boy was certain; 'There is someone, I know there is; it looks like a girl with long reddish-gold hair!' Then hardly knowing what he did, he raised his arm and waved. At that moment the sun dazzled his eyes, and when he looked again the figure he thought he had seen was gone. Whittle maintained he couldn't have seen anyone from that distance and it must have been a trick of the light, but Boy was adamant, insisting that he had for an instant seen a golden-haired girl looking down at him.

'Maybe it was a fairytale Princess,' Whittle remarked in jest.

'Who is in charge of the Palace when the King is away?' asked Boy.

'The Queen, of course,' replied Whittle. 'Queen Constance is the perfect wife for his Majesty the King. I've heard she takes great pride in her ability to organise every detail of life within the Palace. She is in sole charge of everything that happens in the Court from day to day. The courtiers, attendants, ladies in waiting, servants, and all those who prepare the food, clothing and gifts, and see to the comfort of visitors, are answerable to her alone.'

'She must be very busy for a Queen,' mused Boy, 'I always thought they just sat on a throne every day wearing their crowns.'

'Not Her Majesty,' replied Whittle stoutly, 'she supervises the running of the entire royal household, deciding who is in favour at any particular time, and which nobles, courtiers and wise men are chosen to attend royal banquets. Yet even though she is middle-aged, she still wears her hair long and looks very beautiful, and they say she is charming and gracious in all her ways.'

He went on to explain to Boy how burdened with duties the King was, that as an absolute, all-powerful ruler he had to oversee and make decisions on every aspect of the country's government. When he was in residence at the Royal Court, Ministers, Advisers and Members of the High Council would attend audiences to discuss matters with him at scheduled times each day. Additionally, however, affairs of state often took him away from the Palace, sometimes for long periods.

He would make Royal Tours at different times of the year, which covered large areas and meant that he would have to stay at some of the various royal residences scattered far and wide within the Kingdom. Even though the King's State Visit to Carnac lasted only a few weeks, the fact that he was away from his country left many of his subjects with a feeling of loss when their Sovereign was no longer in his realm.

'We will all be overjoyed to see him come home again,' said Whittle, 'and I'll wager he'll be equally glad to get back to his lovely wife and daughter.'

Whether the King was at home or on his travels, under Queen Constance's direction life at the Royal Court was always colourful, elegant and full of interest. The large, spacious rooms were always decorated with rich hangings embroidered with gold and silver thread, and furnished with elegant chairs, tables and couches made of the finest timber, often brought from lands far away and lavishly carved. The Palace formed a superb setting for the nobility and courtiers, all dressed in the finest fabrics that were complemented by the colours of the smart royal livery worn by attendants and servants alike. When meals were served, each one seemed like a banquet. Guests would be served with many courses offering a wide selection of dishes made from the finest, freshest ingredients and complemented by well-spiced mead. While they ate, diners would be serenaded by musicians; afterwards, dancing and other entertainment would be provided.

'All that wondrous world of splendour and opulence high above us,' said Whittle as Boy craned his neck upwards again, 'is a perfect setting for the Royal Family.' Boy was speechless as he gazed at the wonder of it all.

Meanwhile, the Royal Palace was buzzing with activity as everyone was putting the finishing touches to preparations for the King's return. Queen Constance, as usual, kept things firmly under her control, so her daughter Princess Guinevere was able to slip away from her mother and her circle of friends. She was now fourteen years of age, and was beginning to feel the first stirrings of independence. Always a happy-natured girl, she had a great sense of fun, laughing a lot and always ready to play amusing games like dressing up or hide and seek. She had been closely guarded and cared for since birth, and her upbringing in the Royal Palace had left her in ignorance of the outside world, other than what she had learned through visitors or from the children of the nobility who had been chosen to be her friends.

Hardship and pain were unknown to her, yet she was growing up to be a bright, sensible girl who even so retained her free spirit. As she grew, her attitudes were changing, and it was plain to all that the walls of the compound would not contain her curiosity for long. Already, eager to learn more of what the outside world was really like, she would often run up the stairs and out onto the platform which ran along the wooden exterior walls, from where she could lean over and gaze out into the distance. On top of the walls, which were on top of the great mound, itself on top of a natural basin, she felt completely isolated and alone. An intelligent girl, Princess Guinevere was more and more beginning to question what lay beyond the confines of the Palace walls. Even though still only a child, what she really wanted was her own independent life and he own experiences, not just stories that other people told her.

Her father, none other than the great King Arthur himself, was the noblest and most powerful man in his kingdom, and so as his daughter she was a royal Princess and could have virtually whatever she asked for, but still she felt there was something missing. It was the ability to be impulsive and spontaneous, free of court etiquette and duty. Deep down, she knew she had not yet really begun to live. Daydreaming, Guinevere would believe that some day she would meet a young man and they would leave the Palace to start their own life together. Her Prince would be out there somewhere, and she often dreamed that one day he would come to take her away.

As she mused on her longed-for future, Guinevere was looking down on the great crowds which were gathering ready to greet her father the King on his return from overseas. From the great height at which she stood, they looked so tiny, like masses of ants scurrying to and fro. Then suddenly she became aware of one small figure standing on a grassy bank at the back of a section of the crowd, and as she looked down he raised his arm and waved. Instinctively, she shyly ducked down behind the ramparts and ran away down the stairs. The sudden gesture had startled her, and at first she was angry that one of the common people had dared to salute a Royal Princess! Then her good nature reasserted itself, she became curious about what sort of person that might have been, and before she knew it she was wishing she had returned the compliment and waved back.

An hour later Princess Guinevere joined her mother, Queen Constance, on a platform above the main gates of the Palace, where they sat and watched for the runners who would herald the approach of the Royal cavalcade. They did not have to wait long; eager to be home again, King Arthur was making all speed and soon became visible to them, riding a superb white horse and surrounded by his entourage of courtiers, Ministers, attendants and servants carrying flags and banners.

When they came nearer the crowds began to cheer loudly in welcome, and as the King passed by every man bowed and every woman dropped a curtsey in honour of his presence. Queen and Princess rose to their feet and waved as horns and drums sounded a salute from the high walls. Seeing them, King Arthur stopped, climbed down from his horse and walked the last few yards. At his approach the great main gates opened and the Queen and Princess, who had hastened down the stairs from their platform, ran forward into his arms. All thoughts of royalty were forgotten for a long moment: a man was greeting his much-missed wife and daughter. It was good to be back, he thought, with the two most precious people he loved most dearly.

Chapter Five

During the two months following his return, King Arthur managed to clear the backlog of affairs of state that needed his personal attention; any routine matters could be dealt with by his Ministers and the High Council without constant referral to him for a decision. He knew that as an absolute ruler he was only able to delegate a certain amount of administrative work, but his absence overseas, short as it was, had brought home to him how often he was away from his wife and daughter, and how much he missed them. Also, Guinevere at the age of fourteen was now developing rapidly, both in body and mind, and he wanted to be there for her, to provide help and advice through the inevitable difficulties of growing up.

'This winter,' he declared to himself, 'we will leave the Royal Palace and spend time as a family at our Cornish retreat in the far South West. It is warmer there, while Constance and I have much to talk about together. We can do so there undisturbed, and it will be good for Guinevere to leave Court formalities behind and be free to do whatever she pleases. She is after all only a child, and it will be good for her to play naturally and make new friends of her own choosing.'

So they duly travelled west, taking only a few trusted servants and belongings with them. Word had been sent on ahead by Queen Constance to the coastal residence, where a small number of staff and guards were making preparations for their arrival, although they also knew to keep everything as informal as possible.

As the royal party made their way through the countryside, small crowds came out to greet and cheer them wherever they passed. King Arthur was pleased to see how popular he and his family were, and vowed to himself that he would make a point of travelling more among them in his tours around the Kingdom.

Even being so popular however, proved tiring eventually, and the royal family, were very glad to reach their final destination. The winter residence was strategically positioned on a coastal headland surrounded by high cliffs, the only access being a narrow strip of land, which was fortified by a huge wooden wall that was easily defended. They heard the great gates close behind them with a real sense of relief.

In the days and weeks that followed, Guinevere had a wonderful opportunity to rediscover all the secret places she had made her own so often in the past. There was one particular spot on the cliff-top where she could sit out of the wind, warm herself in the winter sunshine and enjoy magnificent views far out to sea, while watching the seabirds swoop and wheel in the air above and around her.

Here Guinevere could believe now and then that she really was flying freely with the birds, as she had thought of doing so often on the ramparts of the Royal Palace which they had so recently left. Thinking of the ramparts reminded her of the strange occasion on the day her father returned, when she had seen a tiny figure raise his arm and wave to her. A Princess grows up believing that all things are possible, and somehow that episode became interwoven in her mind with her thoughts of being carried off to a new, freer life by a handsome Prince.

'Maybe the Gods will make my wish come true,' she said aloud to the birds, 'they can, you know, especially for a Princess.' And she raised her eyes to give thanks to the great Sun God who, although a paler shadow now of his blazing summer glory, was still the all-powerful ruler of the heavens. Then hearing her mother calling, she got up, said goodbye to the birds and ran home to find that food was already being served.

That year the winter was very mild, with many fine days that simply flew past. All too soon, nature was announcing the coming of Spring and it was time for the Royal Family to retrace their steps back to the mighty Royal Palace perched high on its great mountain of earth. King Arthur returned to the audiences with his Ministers and his meetings with the High Council; Queen Constance resumed her supervision of life at Court, checking that no one had become lazy in her absence. Soon the great chambers were humming busily again with activity and the Royal Family's winter retreat idyll became just a treasured memory.

As an experienced ruler of long standing, King Arthur very soon found himself back in his regular royal routine, and assumed that things would continue as they had always done.

But one day an unexpected foreign visitor arrived asking for an audience, and after that things were never to be the same again. As soon as the visitor was shown into the Audience Chamber, King Arthur realised that it was the foreign traveller who had come to speak with him in Carnac. He was the one who had presented him with the wondrous globe which looked like a shining ball of water, and which now had pride of place in his private apartments. Some considerable time had passed since their meeting, yet the King had thought often about the remarkable stranger and was in fact delighted – although royal protocol forbade him to show it – to meet this strange person again.

When the formalities of greeting were over, King Arthur dismissed his attendants; he wanted the two of them to talk freely without being overheard, and sensed that the stranger felt the same. As they began to converse, the King soon realised that they had many thoughts and ideas in common; a strong current of empathy flowed between them.

King Arthur soon became used to the man's strange appearance; of medium height and fair skinned, he always wore a hood made of leather, which he explained was the customary headgear for learned men in his country. As they talked, personal appearances were soon forgotten; the King realised that the stranger had great wisdom, coupled with amazing vision and focus. He spoke of new and exciting ideas, vast projects undertaken in other countries to improve their quality of life. He began unrolling scrolls, opening manuscripts, unfolding drawings and designs to prove his point. King Arthur was astounded at the wealth of diagrams and pictures displayed, many of which he had never seen the like of before.

By the end of their first session they both knew they shared the same interests, and many more such discussions were to follow. They talked for hours, quite often late into the night after the King had finished his essential royal duties, exchanging thoughts and ideas. Their trust in each other developed to the point where their mutual understanding had become virtually unlimited, but above all else it was their great respect for each other that proved a firm and lasting bond of friendship. This was the fertile soil in which progress could grow and flourish, with two such learned and powerful men being able to communicate on such a high level. King Arthur was becoming aware that the two of them acting together could provide the opportunity for him to bring about great forward-looking changes, not just for his own country but possibly for the world.

So engrossing were these new thoughts and ideas that Queen Constance was beginning to find it increasingly difficult to attract her husband's attention. She sensed that the stranger was a good man, and had no cause to dislike him, but inevitably felt somewhat put out by being excluded from these discussions which took up so much of King Arthur's time. However she respected their friendship and understood that great men needed to create; it was part of their make-up. It was just that they had their own way of going about things, and she realised that there was no part for her to play in this process.

The best way she could help them, Queen Constance thought, was to trouble them as little as possible with day to day affairs, and so she decided to devote even more of her time to keeping the organisation of the Royal Court in smooth running order. She could always find something new to keep her busy, and she loved to entertain and be involved with people, creating an atmosphere of laughter and fun which kept everyone happy and in good humour.

The Queen had a strong personality and was fully capable of living her own life independently when necessary; she was not one of those ladies who follow their husbands around in childlike dependency. By the same token, she felt it right that her husband King Arthur should pursue his own aims and objectives without distraction.

Soon the King's interest in the papers and plans the stranger had brought with him, and the suggestions he was making, began to take a more practical turn. Over the following weeks more and more people were being consulted on how a certain unnamed project could be put in hand. Then one day King Arthur instructed that a clearing should be made in the woodlands just a short distance from the Royal Palace.

What it was for, no one was told and no one could discover! Experts were called into his Royal presence and asked how a particular type of wood or stone could be obtained and used for construction, and how earthworks could be built quickly and efficiently, then dismissed without being made privy to what exactly was being planned.

Once the clearing had been made and levelled, building materials were brought to the site and a large work area set out nearby. The most expert craftsmen were called on to stop whatever they were doing and to make themselves available to work under strict instructions from the stranger. This new favourite of the King's had quickly become known as 'The Hawk', because with his unusual headgear, some said he looked like a hunting falcon.

Every day, Princess Guinevere's curiosity drove her to look down over the walls in an attempt to puzzle out what this mysterious construction might be. Indeed, the entire Royal Household was beginning to ask the same question. The High Council, too, inevitably felt that they should be involved in what appeared to be so great a project, but King Arthur explained that it did not concern them at this time. The tide of curiosity was running so high that the King regretfully decided there was only one way to keep the project's progress secret, and that was to build a high fence around the site. Never before had he felt the need to keep something secret from his own people, but this was a more important undertaking than anything he had ever done before, so it was vital that no one should have any idea of what it might be until everything had been completed.

The King was their absolute ruler, and such was the respect and honour in which he was held that no one questioned his decisions. For a whole year, therefore, work went on undisturbed and in complete secrecy behind the high fence surrounding the clearing, despite the fact that it was absorbing all the local skills, resources and stores of building materials. The mystery deepened when several smaller clearings were made in the same area, which it was rumoured were to be used as sites for ovens and furnaces of a size and temperature never before achieved. The Hawk had asked who was the man generally considered to be the country's leading expert on such matters, and the name of 'Old Sniffy' was unanimously recommended.

A real character, 'Old Sniffy' was now getting on in years, but had spent a lifetime using the power of heat to work wonders with making pottery and earthenware, along with many types of metal which he would shape into whatever was required. From a bronze axe to a gold bracelet, Old Sniffy could produce them all. He was bent and stooped from working long hours in confined spaces, and his skin was dry, lined and leathery as a result of years of exposure to searing heat. His exertions in such high temperatures always made him sweat a great deal, and his nose was always running. The inevitably large droplet would form on the end of his nose, resulting in his acquiring the name by which he was now always known; his original one had long since been forgotten, even by Old Sniffy himself.

Working so much on his own had made him a somewhat cantankerous old character, but Old Sniffy soon warmed to The Hawk as one expert to another, respecting his knowledge and fascinated by the new ideas and techniques he was suggesting. It had long been a dream of his to make the hottest furnaces ever known, and here was the stranger suggesting ways he could achieve this, together with new ways of making materials never seen before. Until now only The Hawk and King Arthur had understood these remarkable techniques, and now Old Sniffy was invited to share their knowledge on condition that he was sworn to strict secrecy; no one, not even his own family, must know anything of what they planned. As a true professional, Old Sniffy heartily agreed with this; he had gained his personal experience through his own hard work, and always refused to give his secrets away to others. He thoroughly approved of The Hawk's strict discipline when it came to privacy.

One night while all this was going on, King Arthur was relaxing for a few hours in front of a roaring fire in his private apartments, with Princess Guinevere sitting on the floor beside him while he stroked her long golden hair. Looking into the flames and then up at her father, she quietly asked 'What is going on, Father? You and that man, the one they call The Hawk, are causing something very strange and mysterious to happen. It will affect us all, I can feel it!'

King Arthur smiled down at her and replied 'Yes, that's right, my dear. Something wonderful is happening. I believe that the Gods in their wisdom have chosen me to create a new beginning, to establish a new standard of excellence for all men to follow. I do not fully understand it even now. All I know is that The Hawk and I are causing things to happen, and what is driving us is so powerful that it must be of the Gods. Trust in me as I trust in them, and all will be well. We are on the threshold of a new era, and we are all very privileged to be part of this wonderful time.'

Later that evening, Queen Constance watched her husband walking with The Hawk, deep in earnest discussion. She had warmed to the stranger who was giving the King such strong faith in a better future and showing him how this could be achieved. Her husband was doing what he had been born to do; this deep friendship was proving part of the means whereby he would be able to achieve great things. She felt proud that her Arthur was truly a King, fully capable of taking up a challenge that would bring about rapid progress for the betterment of all his people.

Chapter Six

In the murky darkness that filled the big, windowless room, a single round eye suddenly opened. Liquid and glistening, it shone in the faint, wavering light that came from two tall candles placed on either side of an elaborate shrine set in a large, shadowy niche.

The eye looked hopefully around, swivelling up, down and sideways before deciding that further inspection was fruitless, then promptly snapped shut again.

At that moment the candles, which had been burning feebly, suddenly flared into life, revealing the owner of the eye to be an extremely large, hideously wart-encrusted, slimy toad. The repugnant creature crouched motionless, sat on a silver tray which had been placed on a shelf directly in front of the shrine. It looked as though it had not moved for a very long time, in fact it was difficult to see that it was alive. Only a slow, rhythmic pulsating movement in it's throat showed that it was breathing.

Hard though it was to believe, the toad was the only pet and intimate companion of a fourth member of the Royal Family.

Modred by name, he was King Arthur's nephew, the only son of the King's much-loved sister Olwen who had tragically died in childbirth. She had never revealed who the father was while she was alive, and no one had been able to discover the answer subsequently.

Even while still very young, Modred had proved himself to be a singularly unpleasant child, prone to wild and unruly conduct that swiftly turned viciously violent when his wishes and desires were thwarted. Some suspected that a malignant witch had cursed him at birth; others whispered that his father must have been a creature of darkness from the Underworld who had placed Olwen under an evil spell.

As he grew older, however, Modred proved himself to be cunning as well as evil. He realised that power lay with the King his uncle and that rather than demanding his whims and desires should be fulfilled he obtained better results by being devious and cultivating an air of false bonhomie.

In the depths of his black heart his only aim was to destroy or pervert things to suit his long-term plans, which involved somehow getting rid of his uncle and seizing absolute power for himself. But he quickly became a past master at hypocrisy and deception, concealing his true nature under a veneer of good fellowship, backed by a judicious mixture of flattery and bribery in the right quarters.

His pale, falsely smiling face was framed by long black hair and a carefully trimmed beard. Modred's white face, together with the black garments he always wore, gave him a sensitive, almost priest-like demeanour which put people off their guard and entrapped many into confiding in him. As a result, in addition to being tolerated for King Arthur's sake because of his royal blood, he gradually built up a number of powerful supporters and allies. These were initially drawn from courtiers and minor officials and then as his ability to hoodwink and beguile people increased, he concentrated more on those in higher authority.

An early victim was the High Priest, Efflan himself. This good and holy old man thought so well of everyone that he was completely taken in by Modred's smiling exterior with its façade of feigned good nature and concern. Not for an instant did he suspect his flatterer's true motives, or the cunning with which he schemed and manipulated to twist facts and events to suit his own long-term plans.

Seeing Efflan's acceptance of Modred's involvement in important affairs, others soon followed his example. These included many of the Chieftains and Elders, and eventually even some members of the High Council.

With those of lowlier status, the common people and his own underlings, however, Modred's approach was totally different. Gone were the fawning concern and false bonhomie; intimidation, extortion, threats and even physical abuse took their place. From an early age all his servants lived in deadly fear of his anger; any mistake or accident, however trivial, usually provoked an outburst of terrifying rage followed by severe punishment.

Modred was so feared and detested by the people that no woman would enter his service. He disliked females intensely; as far as he was concerned they were stupid, over-sensitive and totally unpredictable. He never involved them in his plans, only looking upon them as things to be used and discarded.

Male servants, however, were his preferred victims for intimidation and bullying; after all, it was for their own good. When serving him at mealtimes, if a servant was unlucky enough to drop a dish or spill a drop of mead, Modred would order the guards to take him out, then strip and thrash him mercilessly. Such was his warped nature that he would take pleasure in such events and enjoy watching the beatings through a spy-hole in the wall.

It was not Modred's way, however, to carry out any of these evil acts in person; as a royal prince, he considered such conduct beneath him. It was his privilege to give orders and to enjoy the outcome of others' actions. As a result he was always surrounded by a gang of cut-throat ruffians and bully-boys, chief among them being two particular henchmen, Potter and Bullpin. This repellent couple, one short and squat, the other tall and gangling, shared their master's psychopathic tendencies and delighted in carrying out his most perverted orders. They had no hesitation in using their influence or downright intimidation to force people to act in ways which would suit Modred's evil plans, and they had such appalling reputations that few were prepared to refuse any 'requests' they made.

Using these two thugs, Modred was able to influence many things secretly without incriminating himself. All his scheming was based on a strategy of acting covertly, so that if anything went wrong he would not be held accountable and was always able to deny any knowledge of the affair.

Modred's unpleasant attitude and behaviour when young had so appalled Queen Constance that she insisted he should live a good distance away from the Royal Palace, and that there should be no communication between him and the rest of the royal family, particularly the Princess Guinevere.

Initially Modred was furious at being banished from what he considered to be his rightful home, but as his devious mind began to examine the situation he realised that it could actually be turned to his advantage. In his own compound, he would have the ability to plot and scheme without the risk of detection. As for his royal uncle, King Arthur regarded Modred as a pest and a nuisance, but in his view a harmless one, who was in any event best kept out of the way. This became even more necessary after The Hawk's arrival, when he and the King became so totally occupied with their secret project that they wanted no interference from anyone.

So it was that Modred was able, gradually but with growing ease and rapidity, to increase his influence in all aspects of government while the two people with the ability to see through him and his schemes had their attention occupied elsewhere.

In his own domain, Modred was the absolute lord and master in a way he ultimately planned to be throughout the country. While insisting on absolute and instant obedience from all, he remained withdrawn and aloof as an individual. This was largely due to his feelings of overwhelming superiority to other people; at the same time, his growing paranoia made him increasingly suspicious of everyone with whom he came in contact, making him obsessively secret in all his dealings.

No other human being, not even a trusted servant – for Modred trusted no one – was ever allowed to enter his private chamber, which he kept bolted and barred at all times. The only other living occupant of this dark, windowless place was the one creature Modred tolerated as company: the large, repulsive-looking toad that always squatted in front of the shrine. Other, more acceptable pets had been given to him in his youth with the hope that they might help to improve his nature, but the poor animals had suffered his ill-treatment and some of them were eventually found dead, strangled during one of his frenzied rages.

Now the toad was all he had; somehow it had survived over the years, possibly because Modred identified with the toad as being so cold and unfeeling; they suited each other. When the successful outcome of some evil deed had put Modred in a good mood, he would catch large flies and feed them to the creature using a long pair of tweezers. When, more often, he was in a bad mood, the toad would go unfed for weeks or even months, although sometimes it would patiently keep watch for hours and eventually catch a fly itself with a long, sticky tongue that could strike with incredible speed.

Modred thought of his toad as the guardian of the shrine, which contained a large image of Cernunnos, god of darkness and winter barrenness. This fearsome figure, visible only dimly by the light of the candles and partially obscured by their thick smoke, was depicted sitting cross-legged. On his head was a large pair of horns in the form of stags' antlers, so that he appeared half human and half beast. His right hand held a twisted torc or torque similar to the one he himself had on; these were sacred neck-ornaments, worn only by gods and heroes. Cernunnos's left hand grasped a ram-headed serpent, symbolising wisdom, strife and infertility, all attributes of this particular god. Modred revered this 'Lord of Wild Things' as he was both very powerful and very capricious, capable of raising storms and blighting crops if he were crossed in any way. To Modred, this was a power after his own heart, and very often he would dedicate a particularly vile act to Cernunnos.

Once Modred had considered sacrificing the toad to him, but on approaching it with a dagger the creature had instantly opened both its eyes and fixed him with such a fearsome and baleful glare that even Modred had for once stayed his hand. From that moment on he was convinced that the spirit of the god inhabited the toad's body, and began treating it with great care. He was also convinced that Cernunnos regarded him with especial favour, and that with the god's influence his evil plans would come to a successful conclusion.

During all this time he had been secretly undermining people's confidence in the unknown great new project, which so engrossed the King and The Hawk. He subtly planted seeds of doubt in the minds of those with whom he discussed it, without saying anything directly. His meeting with Efflan the High Priest was typical.

As soon as he was shown into the old man's chamber, he began flattering him, saying:

'You are indeed looking well, your Reverence.'

'Thank you, Modred,' Efflan replied, 'what do you want with me?'

'Only,' Modred murmured quietly, with artfully furrowed brow, 'that I feel I should express my concern regarding some members of the High Council. There is a general unease among them with regard to his Majesty's new project, and I was hoping that you could help me, your Reverence, to put their minds at rest over this uncertainty.'

'What is the cause of this "uncertainty" you speak of?'

'Well, your Reverence, would it be possible for you to speak at the Council's next meeting? It would not need to be on any particular subject, but your very presence there would without doubt create a sense of harmony. Your Reverence is, after all, our earthly representative of what the Gods would want for us. Of course if there is anything I can do to support you, I will gladly follow your instructions. It would be very good for the High Council to be given a sense of solidarity and strength, your Reverence.'

Modred knew that Efflan would do as he had suggested. He was diabolically clever at using people without their even realising it. He would play equally on their innocence or loyalty, or whatever he had found to be their weakest and most vulnerable point. Mainly he was a past master at keeping others in a state of blind ignorance, whether it was the Priests, the High Council or the Elders, he ensured that they could only see what he wanted them to see, exactly as he did with the Chieftains from outlying areas. Having cunningly blinkered their vision, Modred was able to make himself seen as a man of undoubted honour and integrity, always acting with the best interests of others in mind.

Such complete control had to be based on the most accurate and up to date information, and Modred had for years been sending out his secret spies as "moles" planted in useful places to glean snippets of knowledge and to find gullible people to befriend. The day to day operation of this intelligence network he left to Potter and Bullpin, who hectored and bullied their hapless victims with great relish, while keeping all decision-making in his own hands.

So cleverly and deviously did he organise this that other people firmly believed he was motivated solely by good intentions. Thanks to his status as a member of the royal family, if anything awkward did come to light he was always prepared to say that he was working on behalf of the King. Knowing that this would never be challenged or, in his mind even better still, he could allow people to think this without committing himself in anyway.

Modred had cultivated this habit of non-involvement, of distancing himself from anything which could reflect badly on him. In addition to having a thoroughly evil and psychopathic mind he was also a coward, unable to confront anyone directly. This was particularly true with regard to the stranger, The Hawk, now in such high favour with the King. Modred hated him for this, fearing his power, seeing him as a potential rival, and feeling that it was his own rightful place to be so much in the Monarch's confidence, not some jumped-up nobody from overseas.

Day by day his resentment was growing and festering, and soon he had become totally obsessed with the question of how to undermine this new threat. Being Modred, all he could think about was how to attack, punish or better still arrange for the man's death.

But while The Hawk's influence was growing with the King, so preoccupied were they that they did not realise to what extent Modred's own undercover influence was increasing, spreading like a cancer festering within the body of the High Council and beyond.

'No one must know the extent of my plans,' he would think to himself, 'I have a great destiny, which the influence of the mighty Cernunnos will help bring to fruition. I am destined to become a King or an Emperor, Ruler of the World. All will have to bow and pay homage to me and me alone!'

No one could tell from his smooth, bland, hypocritically friendly exterior what was going on in Modred's black heart. In the seething, boiling cauldron of his warped mind, monstrous schemes writhed and twisted. Not a single person was aware how far advanced his psychopathic insanity had grown, or what terrible events lay in store for the royal family and all who lived on the Isle of Breton.

Chapter Seven

It was a fine, sunny morning. Princess Guinevere had woken early and felt full of energy, so she dressed quickly, not bothering to plait her hair, which shone like the colour of rose-gold in the morning light. She slipped out of her room without any of her attendants noticing, hurrying along the passage and climbing quickly up the steps to the platform which ran along the inside of the Palace's huge outer defences.

Here she had a favourite viewing place; it was where she had looked down on the boy who had waved to her on the day of her father's return from overseas. Now, her gaze was directed outwards and onwards, as she surveyed the far horizon, her face to the morning breeze, looking dreamily into the distance.

Guinevere's thoughts were far away, but she suddenly came out of her reverie as she heard footsteps approaching softly from behind. Turning quickly round, she saw a man standing respectfully a little way from her. It was her father's friend, the one they called The Hawk.

Seeing her turn, the man bowed low.

'Greetings, Princess Guinevere!' he began, smiling reassuringly as he spoke. 'I hope you will forgive my approaching so quietly, but I saw you were deep in thought and did not want to startle you.'

'You must be wondering what the King your father and I have been doing that is so secret,' he added.

'All I have heard,' replied Guinevere 'is that you are the stranger whom nobody knows. The only thing that anyone knows for certain about you is that you have found favour with my father the King.'

The Hawk was much taken aback by this answer. The very regally self-possessed – and beautiful – young girl before him showed no fear at being alone with him, and her royal training was keeping her curiosity in check, but she was still very young and obviously wanting to know more about him. The Hawk looked deep into her green eyes, at the level gaze with which she regarded him, smiled again and proceeded to explain matters to her.

'I would like to be your friend, Princess,' he began.

'Who are you, then?' Guinevere burst out impetuously, 'everything you do is so mysterious!'

'My name is Merlin; they called me a Hawk, so I have decided to adopt the name – it's the name of a Falcon!'

'Mmm – "Merlin" – yes,' reflected Guinevere thoughtfully, 'I like that name, it suits you.'

'I am glad you approve, Princess,' replied Merlin solemnly, bowing low again. 'I come from a land far away across the sea, a land of many lakes and rivers where men travel in boats from house to house. The people from where I was born have for generations been keepers of ancient knowledge. Alchemists specialise in turning things that are of no value into things which are highly prized; we are renowned for discovering new methods and new ideas. Others like myself specialise in mathematics and sacred geometry – the art of working with numbers and drawings and using them to create all kinds of useful objects and devices. There are many more subjects, too, which all combine into a great pool of knowledge. We have been able to preserve and keep alive many branches of learning, which have been useful to many countries throughout the world.'

Despite his friendliness, Guinevere found herself questioning this man Merlin who seemed so learned. She was still doubtful, but managed to summon up enough courage to ask:

'If there is such a vast store of knowledge in your own country, why have you come to my Father's land and what are you planning to do here?'

'Ah,' Merlin replied, 'I have come here to help your father the King to discover his true self. I believe that with my help he will become one of the greatest men who ever lived.'

Guinevere had heard many legends and tales in which men had to fight battles in order to become powerful, but Merlin seemed to be a man of peace. So she asked:

'Do you intend to kill anyone to achieve your aim?'

'No,' he said earnestly, 'that is not my way. I only bring good. If – and the Gods are willing – your Father and I complete our task, it will prove to be of great benefit to all humanity.'

'All this is very grand talk,' thought Guinevere, 'but are your plans just wishful thinking?' So she replied in a somewhat haughty tone, 'These are surely rather boastful words from a stranger to our country! Even though you have obviously won over my Father, I am still not entirely sure that I can trust you.'

'Talk in itself is meaningless, Princess,' agreed Merlin, 'so to convince you that I am not just an old man making a worthless speech, I invite you now to accompany me down to the compound below, as proof of my good faith. I have chosen you to be the first person to see the completion of this stage of the work, which has been kept secret until today.'

They walked together out of the main gate leaving the Palace and down to the clearing in the woods below. When they came to the outer fence of the compound, Merlin opened the gate for the Princess to enter. Sensing that she was somewhat nervous, he reassuringly walked ahead of her. Guinevere followed him, although she was momentarily frightened until she looked to see what was now before her. The sight brought her abruptly to a halt.

Rooted to the spot, transfixed with amazement and awe, she gasped 'What ... what is it?'

'It is a dream come true,' said Merlin softly.

Before them rose a beautiful circular building, but it was unlike any other building Guinevere had ever seen before. She tried in her mind to find words to describe it, but was unable to do so, although she felt instinctively that this was a wonderful place in which everything was of the highest quality.

The exterior, which was both round and pointed, had a roof covering made from overlapping wooden tiles so closely fitting that it resembled a giant pine cone which came right down to the ground. This, she thought, looked so magical that the only way she could describe it to herself was to say that it looked as though it had been made by fairies!

'Oh, it's truly wonderful!' she cried, 'Do tell me what's inside, Merlin?'

'I can do better than that; come inside and see for yourself!'

Once inside, Guinevere was again rendered speechless by the spacious beauty of the building's interior. Inside was a large circular room, surrounded by a ring of large stones. These stones supported the roof, while around the outside of the main room were a series of small rooms radiating from the central space.

The carefully worked and cut stone glittered and twinkled in the light that shone down from the opening in the apex of the roof. The thought of magic and a fairy-ring came into her mind as she looked at the stone circle. But by far the most outstanding thing was the woodwork, made from the finest quality timber and polished to the highest degree, which gleamed from the floor up to the spacious roof beams. In fact everything about the building was in perfect proportion and balance; she had never seen anything like it before.

When she had got her breath back, Guinevere eagerly asked, 'Tell me, Merlin, why did you build this beautiful house?'

'Aha,' said Merlin, 'as you have found, it would be impossible to describe in words. Now, I can show it to the

High Council and explain to them some of my plans which your father the King and I intend to propose for the future. This work or undertaking is so different from anything ever achieved before that it will only be possible if we all work together. Your father cannot command that this be done; it will have to be decided upon by the people collectively. You see, the thing is, the building that stands before you, magnificent as it is, is only a small version, a replica, of part of a greater plan that will involve building a much, much bigger structure. It will be the most magnificent building in the whole world.'

Princess Guinevere was so amazed that she wasn't able to take everything in. It was all she could do to whisper, 'How can this be possible?'

Then, to her great joy, Merlin said gently, 'I wanted to show this building to you first, because your Father has agreed that I can give it to you to be your very own house, and you can come here as often as you like!'

Then he added, 'I must go now, but if I need to visit the house, it will be only with your Royal Highness's permission.'

'Oh,' cried Guinevere joyfully, 'thank you, thank you, Merlin! You would not believe how much I have wanted something to call my own. I can now see why you and my

Father are such good friends!' Forgetful of all royal protocol, she gave Merlin a big, heartfelt hug.

Before taking his leave, Merlin emphasised reassuringly, 'Remember that this is your house and no one will ever take it away from you.'

When he had gone, Princess Guinevere spent a long time happily exploring her new house. First she walked around the outside of the structure again, admiring its beautiful shape. Then she gave the interior a thorough inspection, particularly admiring the workmanship in the series of small rooms that opened off the large central open space. Everywhere the wooden floor had been polished until it glowed, and the finish of all the detail was exquisite.

Overjoyed, she stood in the centre of her fairytale house and twirled round and round with her arms outstretched; this, she knew, was one of the happiest moments of her whole life.

Chapter Eight

After the many months of hard work, involving all the planning, and overseeing of the construction, Merlin had felt pleased by Princess Guinevere's intuitive understanding and keen appreciation of his achievement.

'But,' he reflected to himself when back in his room, 'she is an amazingly intelligent girl. I know full well it will not be easy for the people of Breton as a whole to grasp and come to terms with the full implications of all that is involved. While I have, I believe, done all in my power to initiate the process in such a way as to ensure the best outcome for all concerned, much of the planning is so complex that there is no chance of my being able to explain all the details concerning the mysteries and wonders which will remain forever beyond their understanding. After the Elders have seen the smaller version of the building I will give them sufficient time to discuss it among themselves, but will they have the vision really to understand the magnitude of what I am proposing?'

King Arthur was also aware of the difficulties he and Merlin faced. He had already discussed the project and its implications personally with all his closest friends and chief advisers, including most of his Ministers and members of the High Council individually, collectively and at length.

He felt he could best help Merlin by showing everyone that the entire weight of his Royal authority was behind the progress of this project, but in the knowledge that it could only move forward with his subjects' unconditional agreement. This was why he devoted so much of his time to explaining things to them, because in this particular case they had a right to question or even to object to anything regarding the plans he was proposing for the future.

Those with whom the King had spoken would in turn be discussing the matter in confidence with others, and introducing yet more people to this new-found knowledge. Everyone who had seen the replica of the great building, and been told how it would work, would see the tremendous benefits which would flow from having a 'Centre of Excellence'. At the same time, all those consulted had agreed that the right location for such a monumental structure would be where the Summer and Winter Solstices connect.

King Arthur truly believed that their great undertaking was being created with Divine guidance. To him the sacred geometry and the elaborate calculations, which Merlin called "Mathematics", came from within the Spirit of Nature itself.

He also believed the project was unique; 'Merlin has sworn to me,' he told Queen Constance one evening, 'that nothing concerning the concept or design of the great building has come from anyone else. Nor has even he, wise though he is, personally created it. What he says is that he has "discovered it" and that it had existed somewhere else, he only unlocked its secret.'

'Deep words indeed,' murmured Queen Constance, 'but I am sure we can rely on Merlin, even though we cannot fully understand him. If anyone can bring this into being, you and he working together will find a way.'

'Thank you, Constance,' said King Arthur, deeply moved by his wife's total belief in the project.

Meanwhile Merlin was deep in thought, pondering the next practical step to take. The knowledge he had absorbed, and the great discovery he had made, had taken many years to acquire and understand.

'How,' he thought in a rare moment of doubt, 'can even King Arthur, let alone the entire nation fully understand the sheer enormity of what is beginning to take shape? Even I find myself baffled at times.'

Yet his ultimate goal was that, if monarch and people alike had faith and followed the path he had indicated, they would have the rare privilege of seeing the final outcome.

It was, however, for the people collectively to decide their own future. Merlin therefore decided that the next practical step in helping them to a fuller understanding would be to arrange for select groups of four or five members of the High Council at a time to be shown and guided through every aspect of the new building.

'I shall have to do this myself,' thought Merlin, 'and explain the details of the final construction and also explain the structure, otherwise they will only see the outward form and depart not fully aware of all that it symbolises for the future.'

As a courtesy to a member of the Royal Family, it was reluctantly decided that Prince Modred should be given a place in one of the select groups. Unsure of what to expect, he cunningly decided not to follow his usual tactic of lording it gracelessly over all and sundry, but instead to blend quietly into the background and see what he could learn and afterwards turn to his own advantage. During Merlin's guided tour, therefore, he was hardly noticed by the others, and Merlin had no contact with him other than a very formal greeting on his arrival.

As it happened, Modred was completely fascinated by what he saw. Initially his reaction was one of furious jealousy that as a member of the royal family he had not been consulted at the outset. The idea that something so amazing had been created without his knowledge, made his black heart seethe and boil with rage.

Then his devious mind took over, his anger subsided and he began mentally to take over the project for his own purposes.

'Calm down,' he whispered to himself, 'don't let anyone suspect that this has all been conceived and built just for me. For me! Prince Modred the Great! I will get my revenge on that "know it all" Merlin by revealing to the people one day that it is my destiny to rule them from this place! Its magnificence will be worthy of me and show the world my glory!'

He began to weave all these changes into his own plans, and became lost in thought, considering how he would lie low for now, let the project go ahead to completion, and then seize everything for himself. As he left the building it was with a smile on his lips, but a bubbling turmoil of evil thoughts was raging in his warped mind.

When all the highest dignitaries had viewed the building and had sufficient time to explain the concept to others, King Arthur issued a proclamation commanding that a grand meeting of the Elders, High Council and Chieftains should take place. So many would be attending that the Great Meeting Hall of the High Council would be packed to capacity and it was agreed that it might prove necessary for some to be given places outside. Arrangements had been made well in advance for the Great Hall to be prepared and for supplies of food and drink to be available for all those attending over a period of several days.

The most senior Elder, named Durrel, was respected and honoured above all the others. It was he who was naturally called upon to address all present at this very large and extremely important meeting. Whittle, as the recently-elected Chieftain of his tribe, was naturally among them. He was very proud to be the chosen representative of his people, and he felt greatly honoured to be present on such an occasion. He also found himself still very much in awe of his fellow-Chieftains and all the other dignitaries who had come together in the Great Hall.

When eventually all were seated, Whittle looked around at the impressive sight presented by their serried ranks. Everyone looked so different, too, he noticed; people he thought he knew well were no longer immediately recognisable with their fine clothes and clean looks. Some had removed much of their facial hair, so nothing now lay between them and their true, honest selves; it was a good tradition, he said to himself; they could not hide behind their beards now, he thought.

Then a sudden movement caught his attention as Brenon the High Chieftain rose to his feet, raised his hands and waited for everyone to fall silent. Brenon then invited Durrel to address the meeting. After thanking him, the old man started to speak.

'You have all come here today,' he began, 'as representatives of all our tribes from every part of the country. It is important for you to realise that each one of you is an integral part of what is happening here today. This is the beginning of the greatest endeavour that has ever been undertaken by anyone.'

'Many of you may not fully comprehend what we propose, but I tell you this: there has been more energy and power of foresight put into this than anything undertaken before. All our wisest and greatest scholars have been astounded by what is to be revealed. I ask you all to give your total attention to the words that will be spoken here today. There is only one man who is able to speak with the weight and authority the situation demands. I ask you all to rise for His Majesty King Arthur!'

A sudden buzz of surprise filled the Hall for an instant after Durrel had finished speaking. It was unheard of for the King to speak in a meeting! Suddenly outside the Hall drums began to beat, and a fanfare of horns announced that the Royal arrival was imminent.

97

When King Arthur entered the Hall, resplendent in his royal robes of state and his gold crown, and sat in the Seat of Honour, first the Elders rose and bowed low then all the rest of the gathering followed suit.

Once they were seated again, the King began to speak, saying: 'Let me begin by saying I am proud to be your King. It is an honour and a privilege to speak before you all, for you will, I trust, be the ones to carry out my Royal will and act as my strength, so that the entire nation will be united solidly in undertaking the task that lies ahead.'

A low murmur of support ran round the crowded Hall, in which Whittle joined; when it had subsided, King Arthur continued, declaring: 'We are here today to go forward together as one nation, one body and one mind. What I ask is that you work in unity, love and spirituality. We are destined to construct a magnificent building of great size, which will become what I can only describe as a "Centre of Excellence". It will tax all our resources and ingenuity to build, testing our strength and courage to the absolute limit. Once completed, the building will astound the world, for it is as close to the Gods as anything can be.'

He paused for a moment and then went on: 'I ask you to do this as an offering to the Gods, because I am your King and my authority is only of this world. I therefore ask you to join me in this greatest adventure of a lifetime. It is our privilege, as a nation and as a people, that our achievement shall never be forgotten. The Gods be with you all!'

When the King had finished speaking there was total silence for a short time while all present considered the implications of his words. Then Durrel pronounced: 'All rise; the King has spoken!'

Next to speak was Efflan, the High Priest. He stood on the platform to address the meeting, resplendent in his ceremonial robes, and declared 'You may all be thinking that we are planning to build a House of the Gods. That is not so. It is true that the building will be so magnificent that the Gods can be represented within it, but we do not know and can never understand their purposes; all we mortals can do, with all our hearts and minds, is our very best.

'In truth, this building will be for the King; it will represent both his authority and his love for you, his subjects. We intend to build it in the sacred place that we already know is closest to the Gods, where the Solstices meet.

'There should be no doubt in our minds; it is the will of the Gods that we construct this building. Not just for all represented here today and their families, but for our ancestors and for all our children yet to be born.' Efflan paused for a moment. 'The Gods be with you all!'

When Efflan had finished and resumed his seat, it was the turn of Brenon the High Chieftain to bring this part of the meeting to a close.

'You have heard the words of King Arthur,' he cried, 'you know his will and what he asks of you. It is now the time to ask questions, debate and argue among yourselves. You must come to a unanimous decision. This great undertaking cannot proceed unless everyone is united together in one spirit. His Majesty will now retire, and when you are of one accord, he will return to hear your decision.'

Chapter Nine

Decision-making was expected of a Chieftain, and those who were chosen by their fellow-tribesmen took their responsibilities very seriously. As a result, every topic put to them for discussion was debated with the utmost sense of importance. Whether it was a routine boundary dispute or a subject which would vitally affect everyone's future – such as now, when they had to decide whether to proceed with a full-scale version of the revolutionary new building created by King Arthur and Merlin – it had to be deliberated and evaluated at length. All the evidence had to be looked at in great detail, which would subsequently mean many discussions.

Some of the Chieftains, Whittle among them, went in small groups to view the exact scale replica building for themselves, and then reported back to the others. All this took time, so food and drink were always on hand as an essential part of the proceedings.

Refreshments helped to provide a focal point for gatherings, bringing people together to make good use of them and keep their strength up while arguing long into the night. This was all part of the Chieftains' traditional way of fully understanding matters about which they were being asked to make decisions. If they considered something together, it would then be easier to come to a unanimous decision.

To assist their deliberations, the Chieftains sent an invitation to Merlin, asking if he would appear in person to answer their questions. He replied that nothing would give him greater pleasure, and at the appointed time he entered the Great Hall and stood before them.

A low murmur of surprise ran round the assembled ranks of Chieftains. This was not the quietly-dressed, scholarly person they had seen accompanying King Arthur. Now, Merlin was wearing a long, deep purple cloak, embroidered in gold thread with strange symbols and designs that no one had seen before. His headgear was no longer the familiar leather hood, but one so closely worked with rich silver embroidery that whenever he moved his head it glittered in the light like a helmet.

This created a powerful effect, heightened even more by the staff Merlin carried, which was obviously a symbol of great authority. At the top of the staff the wood had a natural twist, into which had been fitted a glittering quartz crystal, which again was something never before seen by his audience. To them it looked like a piece of ice that somehow refused to melt, as did the small gleaming ball hanging from his shoulder on a long thin cord. Here before them, they all realised, was a man of great wisdom, power and authority.

'Greetings to you all,' began Merlin, raising his staff in salute to all areas of the Great Hall in turn. 'I thank you for your invitation, and have gladly come to help your deliberation in whatever ways I can.' Merlin paused for a moment, then continued: 'Many of you will already have heard of me, although I would imagine that some very strange stories have been told about me, which may have given you a false impression of why I came here.' He paused again. 'To put your minds at rest, I shall tell you the truth. I am here to serve King Arthur; I have sworn allegiance to him and his realm. I have no influence over your King; I am here only to advise him at this important time.'

'What I have to offer is knowledge; what you do with it is your affair and will be your decision alone. I will assist and guide you all I can, but let no one say that I have any shred of self-interest at heart. My primary purpose is to help you all, and to ensure that you as inhabitants of the Isle of Breton evolve into one of the greatest nations in the history of mankind.'

'I know it is always difficult to trust a stranger,' Merlin went on, 'that is only human nature. But trust will come, I am sure, as we hopefully move forward together in this great enterprise, the future of which is now in your hands.'

'Let me tell you now, though, progress will not be easy; every aspect of the project will be difficult both physically and mentally. This vast undertaking will tax your spirits to the utmost, but if you have faith and courage, we will prevail and all our efforts will be rewarded.'

As a result of his plain speaking and honest approach, Merlin sensed that at this point the mood of the meeting had swung in his favour. He then called for questions, and went on to answer them all as best he could. To many there were no easy responses; for those individuals who still could not grasp the purpose of the building, or the higher goals it would achieve, he explained that the structure was intended to create a sense of mystery and wonder. Simple explanations just could not be given about everything to everyone.

Indeed the building had been deliberately designed in such a way that it would be impossible for anyone walking inside to fully comprehend its meaning, influence and power. The precise objective behind its creation would be to stir the senses of all those who entered and to make them realise just how little they knew of what the Gods could achieve, and of the vast power and scope of their authority over all things.

This lengthy question and answer session inevitably went on long into the night. Merlin was pleased, and he did not begrudge his time, because the main objective at this stage was to build up the Chieftains' faith in themselves and their own ability to see the project through. He sensed that collectively they were becoming more and more determined to do so.

He finished by saying, 'We have had a full, frank and extremely fruitful discussion, and I thank you all again for your time and patience. Let me sum up in a few words: this great building has been designed as a place where the impossible can be possible. Once it is completed it will stand as enduring proof that absolutely anything is possible where the Gods are concerned.'

Then he bowed low and withdrew.

The Senior Elders, members of the High Council and the assembled Chieftains, Whittle among them, were silent for quite a while as each man and woman took time mentally to consider for themselves the full future implications of the lofty goal which Merlin had so eloquently explained.

Whittle found himself thinking, 'It's not just a building he's been talking about, it's the power to develop ourselves as a nation so that we can build much more than a great hall, however magnificent; we will be building a better future for everyone, especially those who come after us. I like the sound of that; it makes good sense to me.' But even though he was still a new member of the elected Chieftains, he knew better than to make up his mind too swiftly.

Once they all felt they had absorbed Merlin's speech thoroughly, the debate began in earnest. Initially opinions were divided; some were eager to seize any new idea, while others were thinking more of the practical implications and effects.

'The scaled down structure which stands yonder in the clearing,' said one, 'has already cost many hours of hard labour, taken large numbers of our people from their daily tasks, and been a heavy drain on vital materials. If we were to agree to go ahead with a full-sized version, surely it would become so involving and time-consuming that all other work throughout the length and breadth of the land would virtually cease, leaving us and our families to suffer accordingly. Would that not be so?'

'But we cannot stand still, and just muddle on with things exactly the way they are,' said another, 'it is true that King Arthur rules us wisely and we are more prosperous than in days gone by, yet we need to progress to prosper in the future. Such a great project would be the best possible proof to the world at large – but above all to ourselves – that we are capable of doing things that will be of the most benefit to all.'

'I agree with that,' said Whittle firmly; 'as a family man, I want a better future for my children, however good things may seem at the moment. But nothing stands still, and to go forward is always to take chances.'

'No man, not even a wise ruler like King Arthur, can know the future; that is for the Gods to know. Maybe, then, this man Merlin has been sent to us by the Gods as a sign that we have their blessing to proceed. I for one believe in what he says; he talks well, and has great knowledge of things beyond our own understanding. With his guidance, and with the faith to see things through, I say we should give our approval.'

As he finished speaking, there were murmurs of agreement from those around him, but many others still held a more cautious view. Indeed, the debates and discussions continued for another three days, allowing everyone the opportunity to speak his or her mind. Only when all the questions had been asked and all opinions sought did Brenon, the High Chieftain, send word to the Royal Palace that they had reached a unanimous decision.

The whole meeting reassembled the following morning and took their places once again in the Great Hall under Brenon's supervision. All remained seated in complete silence until the drums and horns sounded their royal salute once again.

Then King Arthur entered, robed and crowned as before, followed by Efflan the High Priest and Merlin. All three came to a halt in the centre of the chamber and raised their right arms in salutation. Not a word was spoken. Then all the assembled Elders, High Council and Chieftains rose to their feet and bowed to the King. In his role as High Chieftain, Brenon acted as their spokesman.

'Your Majesty King Arthur,' he announced formally, 'we have come to a decision.' Then, raising his voice, he called out: 'All those in favour raise your right hands and stand up.' In one movement the whole assembly rose to their feet, raised their hands and cheered: 'Arthur! Arthur! Arthur!' Brenon then raised his staff of office, and all fell silent once again.

King Arthur rose to address them, a ringing note of triumph in his voice, saying 'Now we are all together, nothing can stand in our way! Rejoice, I say, rejoice, for we are one in the spirit!' He then bowed ceremoniously to the assembly and, followed by Merlin and Efflan, left the Great Hall to the stirring sound of drums and horns.

That night, in the King's private apartment, Arthur and Merlin dined alone, to celebrate the successful outcome of the great debate. Even now, still slightly surprised at the unanimity of the favourable verdict, he said, 'Merlin, do you realise what we have achieved this day?'

'Absolutely!' smiled Merlin in reply. 'We, my royal friend have together made a decision which has been agreed unanimously by the assembly in the Great Hall on behalf of all your subjects.'

'Our friendship, and ability to work together, has resulted in universal approval to proceed with what will become one of mankind's greatest achievements. As individuals, we would have found the project impossible to realise, but we met and found ways to understand each other. Now, together, we have initiated something that will astound the world.'

'People will remember the names of King Arthur and Merlin for many generations to come; the outcome of this successful decision today will last for hundreds and, possibly, even thousands of years. Someone in the far distant future will see and understand that there must have been a terrific bond of friendship between us for all this to have happened.'

'Who will that person be, I wonder? I cannot tell, but, he or she will understand just as we do. Time is no barrier to the intellect! So, my King, my friend, I give you a toast – to the one who is not yet born, but is with us in spirit, even as we speak!'

Chapter Ten

Once the decision had been taken to proceed with the great building project, the whole kingdom was soon humming with activity. In the following months a great search was begun to find the very best craftsmen and artisans from all over the country. Only those exceedingly gifted would be chosen by their Chieftains to be put forward for this tremendous undertaking. There was an especial need for experienced woodsmen and carpenters, experts at tree felling and timber splitting. Also in demand were people who could be trusted to select which types of wood should be chosen for particular uses, experts in knowing how to read the grain of trees.

Similarly the most expert stone workers would be required, whose families for generations had had experience in quarrying, moving and dressing great boulders. Also, as there would be a need for moving huge amounts of soil, involving having it excavated and transported considerable distances, skilled earthmovers would be another group in great demand.

In addition to these, other highly trained specialists were needed, including rope makers and basket weavers. Lacking any sophisticated forms of technology, the successful progress of the project would depend on the ingenuity, determination and sheer hard work of the chosen band of craftsmen and the will to succeed of their supporting workers.

The entire population had become caught up in the enthusiasm of their Chieftains for the great work that was soon to be undertaken. Throughout the land, people were volunteering in droves, sacrificing their own interests and even their livelihoods in a desire to contribute towards something they believed to be more important than anything else. The response was, therefore, far beyond anything anyone could have imagined. Many had been chosen by their Chieftains, but some determined craftsmen turned up on their own initiative.

On one particular day, for example, a band of seven men arrived to offer their services. Their spokesman announced: 'We have come here to give our all for the cause; we will work harder than anyone else!'

'Who are you?' asked the man in charge of selection, appointed by the High Council, 'and where are you from? You do not speak like local men.'

'We are from the High Northlands,' was the proud response.

'You have indeed come far to answer our call, but why should you be chosen? Indeed, is not one of you a foreigner?' His dress marks him out as different from the rest.

'I will speak for myself,' interjected a strongly built, fair-haired man who towered above his companions – some six feet six inches tall, the man questioning them estimated him to be – a giant of a man with bulging muscles to match.

'My name is Magnus,' he continued, 'I come from a land in the Far North, and I have travelled here because I believe the Gods have ordained it; I come with the spirit, you can see I am strong – if you can use an ox, why not use me?'

Then the man in charge turned to the smallest member of the group, who was barely five feet tall.

'Strength we can use, but what do you think you can do?' he asked, with a hint of sarcasm in his voice.

'I can give my life to this cause,' replied the short young man, 'for I believe the Gods have chosen me to serve; indeed I would be happy to die, if necessary. All of us are of like mind; we have come to work hard, and we work as a team. You will not be disappointed in us.'

Such men were put through a selection process before being chosen to work on the building. If they proved themselves, they would be allocated to a team; if they did not make the grade, they would be told to leave.

Skilled women, too, were sometimes also chosen to join the men at their tasks. One who came to offer her expertise was named Reann; somewhere in her middle years, she was still strong and had an amazing ability to cut and work with stone. Her father had been the most famous of all stoneworkers in his day; he had taught her all he knew, and he had trained her well. She had proved an apt pupil, with an inherited gift for application, and soon became famous in her own right. With her experience, she could make the hard and sometimes dangerous work of stone cutting look easy.

One very special and highly secret gift her father had passed on to her was the ability to move stones of any given size. This was a method, he told her, called "shinffing". She would use levers and blocks to move massive stones and she could even turn these large stones over on her own if necessary. Reann had spent all her time, since she grew old enough to work, in carving, cutting, scraping and polishing stones. Most of this was done out in the open air in all weathers; as a result, her hands had become so rough they looked like crocodile skin, while her face was as brown, lined and weather-beaten as though made of leather.

She was unanimously chosen to be in charge of all stonework, being the only person capable of selecting, organising and instructing a team that would quarry and prepare the stones, ready for moving.

One of the members of the selection team charged with recruiting the most skilled craftsmen in their various fields was Bracken, Whittle's predecessor as Chieftain. His experience and wisdom, gained over many years, coupled with his knowledge of the local area, meant that he knew all the problems which had to be overcome, including the need to find a site which could provide the right types of stone in sufficient quantity. An even bigger problem, once they were located, was how to transport the stone to the chosen site, the point where the Solstices connected. How would this be possible? With his deep belief in the great project, Bracken was convinced that somehow all these obstacles would eventually be overcome. He trusted in the Gods; they would help them find the answers.

Knowing Whittle's lifelong familiarity with the surrounding terrain, Bracken arranged that his successor should be put in charge of the team tasked with locating and transporting the stones. Whittle accepted gladly, but realised that, before he set out, he would have to familiarise himself with the various types of stone he might encounter so that he could be sure they selected the right ones.

Reann explained things to him. 'Quality is the main thing to look for,' she emphasised, 'we need stone that is tough, strong and resistant to the elements. It must be hard-wearing, and the harder the better, as what we are creating is to last for ever.'

'What, then, is the best type to look for?' asked Whittle.

'Avoid limestone at all costs,' replied Reann, 'it is far too soft. Look for granite; that is the best choice. And you will need to find plenty of it; we want large quantities of big stones. Don't consider the stones in the riverbed, for example, they aren't big enough. Search the land for outcrops of rock; if you find some on the surface, it will be a sign that much more lies under the ground which can be quarried out. But, be warned! Yours is a difficult task, and you may have to travel far and search long and hard to track down what we need. The Gods go with you!'

Before setting out, Whittle told Boy of his assignment and the many difficulties he would have to face.

Boy listened intently; 'it will be hard work indeed, Father,' he agreed. At the same time his astute mind was already thinking ahead. If his father and the team did find the right type of stone, they had obviously not fully considered how they would lift and transport them all the way up to the chosen site on top of the high plain. Big stones of the required size would be incredibly heavy; they would surely be unable to drag them any distance, let alone lift them.

'There must be an answer,' thought Boy, so when Whittle and his team had left on their quest, he decided to go and check out the territory himself, tackling the problem from the other side. One thing stood out, he decided, the main problem in bringing stones back from the direction they had taken would be to manoeuvre them up the steep gradient of the escarpment which rose abruptly from the low levels to the high plain.

'How can anyone do this!' he thought despairingly.

Boy considered this dilemma long and hard during the weeks while Whittle and his team were away, but no solution presented itself.

When they returned, the news was not good either. They had literally looked high and low, thoroughly searching the high plain itself and scouring the low levels around the base of the escarpment. As well as looking for stones on the ground, they had followed Reann's advice and dug under the surface to see if there were more, and if they were big enough to use.

It had been an arduous task, but a necessary one. They had searched and dug high and low, sometimes exhausted by their efforts, but it was all to no avail. Very little suitable stone existed where they had searched, and it was certainly not enough for their needs. It was a very depressed and disheartened team that returned to report their lack of success to Reann, Bracken and the High Council. How could they tell Merlin and King Arthur that the first stage of the building project had failed so dismally?

It was then, in his darkest hour, that inspiration suddenly came to Whittle. Perhaps they had been looking in the wrong places, too close to home! He remembered a distant area he had visited many years ago, some twenty miles or more away on the other side of the great wide valley that ran from east to west, north of the high plain.

Of course – at that time he had seen many large stones lying on the surface, he was sure of it; maybe that area had the stones they were looking for, and there was still a chance of success!

'There is so much at stake,' thought Whittle, 'and everyone is so downhearted, that I don't want to raise false hopes again. I will keep this to myself until Boy and I have visited the place and made certain that the right stones are indeed there, and in sufficient quantity.'

That night they slipped quietly away without being noticed – Whittle having told his wife Jenny what they proposed to do, reassured her they would be safe and sworn her to secrecy – and set out on their vital mission to explore the far side of the great valley.

Chapter Eleven

Hearing a hesitant knock on his door, Merlin called encouragingly, 'Come in, come in!' But there was no response, so he got up from his seat, strode across the room and opened the door. Three big, burly men stood there, all looking somewhat nervous and out of place.

'Don't just stand there,' said Merlin briskly, 'I've been expecting you. Come in!'

They ambled clumsily into the room, looking about them cautiously as they did so. Merlin smiled to himself; some of the tales told about him must be strange indeed, he thought.

'It's alright,' he said calmly, 'I won't put a spell on you and there is no need to worry; I am human, regardless of whatever you may have heard.'

Somewhat reassured, they moved forward and stood opposite the table at which Merlin was working. It was piled with parchments covered in what appeared to be drawings of some kind, but the men could make neither head nor tail of them.

'Now then,' Merlin continued, 'you all know who I am; let me see if I can work out which of you three is which.' He gazed keenly at them in turn, pausing at the eldest.

'Aha,' he said triumphantly, 'you must be Ardel, the most experienced of the foresters?'

The man nodded. In his mid-thirties, he was tall and obviously very strong, with a broad chest and big, brawny arms that looked capable of tearing trees out of the ground. Wearing a brown top, and over it a green, sleeveless coat, with his tall frame and bushy beard, he looked for all the world like a Tree Spirit. Tucked in his broad leather belt was a formidable-looking knife and a beautifully shaped and decorated bronze axe in a leather binding.

'And,' went on Merlin, 'you two are the famous expert woodcutters, the brothers Brad and Hoel?' They also nodded in turn, pleased to be acknowledged with such respect by this man who stood so high in the King's favour.

'But which of you is Brad, and which Hoel?' he queried, 'you both look very much alike to me!'

'I am Brad,' said the man standing nearest to Merlin, 'and I am the elder by two years. We are often mistaken for twins by those meeting us for the first time, although my hair is a darker brown than Hoel's. My brother and I are a team; he takes his instructions from me, and we work as one.'

'Excellent,' replied Merlin, 'you are just the men I need. The reason I have asked you here is to do with moving the stones. I know you are experts on trees, not stones, but I am sure you would agree that one of the greatest difficulties we have is transporting the stones from wherever we find them.' Ardel, Brad and Hoel all nodded again in agreement; like everyone who worked much in the open air, they were men of few words.

'Well,' explained Merlin, 'I have thought of a special plan for moving very large stones. They would be impossibly heavy to lift or drag, and this is where you come in, since the plan involves the extremely skilful use of wood.'

'Let me try to put it simply,' he went on. 'First of all, the nature of weight is important. You know that if you try to lift a tree trunk it is very heavy, but when you roll it along, it moves so easily it seems almost weightless?'

'Aye,' they said in unison, 'that be very true.'

'But,' said Hoel, who had an enquiring mind, 'if at one stage the weight is heavy and the next it isn't, where has that weight gone?'

'Puzzling, isn't it!' Agreed Merlin. 'Actually it is still there, but the weight goes into the ground. This is because when something is round it creates a balance – and that is why it is easier to roll a log than to lift it.'

'But sire,' said Ardel, 'what have logs to do with stones? You certainly can't roll a huge gigantic stone for miles and miles, it would be far too heavy.'

'Just so,' replied Merlin, 'and that is there I believe my plan will provide the answer.'

Then Merlin started to explain his plan to the three expert woodsmen. 'My thought,' he began, 'is not to move the stones by intense physical effort; that would be impossible for any distance and could result in people being maimed or even killed. No, I propose doing it using the art of what I call "design". I therefore propose to construct a large wooden cradle, a Stoneroller, consisting of two halves, into which a stone will be placed. When the stone is securely fastened inside, it will be possible to roll the cradle and stone together across large distances with relatively little effort. So with a little ingenuity we can achieve the impossible!'

Seeing the rather blank looks on his listeners' faces, he produced drawings he had made of the wooden cradle showing how the stone would fit into it, as snugly as a kernel in a nutshell. At first they just could not take in this new idea; to their minds, wood was wood and stone was stone, and the idea that the one could assist the other was beyond their grasp, however clearly Merlin tried to explain it.

'I know it is difficult to take in all at once,' he said understandingly, 'one needs time to think it through. Take these drawings away with you and study them, then try

123

making models of the cradle. You'll find that it needs to be constructed using ten different pieces of wood, two large and eight smaller but varying in shape and size. You will have to work out how everything fits together before you can fully understand how it works.'

'Meanwhile,' he went on, we must think ahead and begin by searching for suitable wood to make the full-size cradle – or should I say roller? This will be your responsibility, Ardel; your expertise is needed in making sure the grain follows along the entire length of the wood, in the direction we want it to go. This is essential; it will give each individual piece its maximum strength. We cannot have any cross-grained wood; it would be too weak for our purposes.'

'I see,' said Ardel, 'and to provide the right type of wood, what size trees would I be looking for?'

'The biggest,' replied Merlin, 'we need the biggest, mightiest trees in all the land. The size of the trees will determine the size of the stones we can move.'

'I know of many good trees,' murmured Ardel reflectively, 'but to locate the giants that you need, will indeed take time. I will have to travel the length and breadth of the land; it will probably be many weeks before I find the right trees.'

He looked troubled, but Merlin quickly intervened, saying: 'Do not think, Ardel, that you will have to travel on foot; I have arranged for you to have a sturdy horse. He will carry you well, and speed you on your way!'

Ardel stammered out his thanks at this, but in his mind he was somewhat uneasy. Horses provided pulling power for moving logs, but he had never actually ridden one before, and felt somewhat nervous at the thought of sitting on one. Fortunately Merlin had already been aware of this problem, and had arranged for Ardel to be given a strong, sturdy mount with an even, easy-going temperament. Even so, he found the art of mounting and dismounting somewhat tricky at first and it took a few falls before he got the hang of it. Soon a bond had developed between horse and rider, and Ardel found he was able to ride with confidence, so that he was now looking forward to his journey on horseback.

He knew that the tallest trees with the most suitable timber were most likely to be found near the centre of the great forest which covered the heart of the countryside. The journey held no difficulties for him; he had more than once found timber for other needs in the area before, and remembered the route.

After a ride of three days he reached the territory occupied by the woodland folk. They were a simple people, not farmers like those occupying the open countryside but living among the trees, with their huts built well camouflaged from prying eyes. They lived off nuts, fruits, berries and roots which the woodland provided in abundance, as well as netting and trapping rabbits, squirrels and other small animals and birds. Though simple, their senses were very acute, and any traveller approaching their territory was seen and shadowed on his journey without his being in the least aware of their presence.

Ardel was riding slowly along the woodland path, when a woodlander suddenly seemed to appear out of nowhere and stood on the path before him. Ardel raised his right arm in greeting, then realised he had met this man before.

'Merrivale, it is I, Ardel,' he called out with a smile. The other started at hearing his name spoken by a stranger, then also realised they had met before. The hospitality of the woodlanders towards visitors who came in peace was well-known, and soon Ardel had dismounted and, leading his horse, walked along beside his friend explaining why he was in the forest and how he came to be in possession of a horse.

Ardel was given food and drink at the woodland settlement, and then the Chieftain arrived to greet him. Ardel explained his mission, and asked him: 'Which is the biggest tree in all your forest?'

'I know it well,' said the Chieftain, whose name was Farrel, 'come, I will take you there!'

The Chieftain Farrel, Ardel and Merrivale set off, accompanied by a number of other woodland folk, male and female, who were intrigued by the horse, Ardel himself and his strange request. They led the way through trees whose branches were in full leaf, so they walked along cool and darkly shaded paths. Then, suddenly, they reached a small clearing; Ardel, stepping into it, was momentarily dazzled by the bright sunlight.

He blinked, and found himself staring up at the mightiest forest giant he had ever seen. It was magnificent; broad, with a girth bigger than four persons could encircle with their arms, and so tall, it soared up into the sky so far that its upper branches were out of sight. It was exactly what they needed, the answer to Ardel's prayers. So moved was he that he reverently approached the tree and embraced it. At this, many of the woodland folk joined him in encircling the massive girth so they could embrace it together.

Ardel then reluctantly took his leave and said goodbye to Merrivale, Farrel and the others, promising to return again soon; he then rode back the way he had come, eager to tell Merlin the good news.

On his arrival at the royal palace he went straight to Merlin and related that he had found the biggest and best tree in all the land. Merlin was overjoyed. His first thought was to tell Efflan, knowing that it was essential for the High Priest to be present at the ceremony when the great tree was felled. The old man was delighted at the news, and eager to make the journey straight away.

'Let us travel there now,' said Merlin, 'we will go with Ardel, and take the brothers Brad and Hoel with us.'

When they had gathered together, Merlin called to Ardel, 'Lead the way, master forester, take us and show us this woodland giant!'

Everyone was eager to see it, so they pressed on apace and the journey was soon completed. On arrival, they found that the ground around the base of the tree had already been cleared. Merlin and Efflan were pleased to see how mighty it really was, towering above them in woodland majesty exactly as Ardel had related. They also felt very honoured that Farrel was waiting to greet them in person.

'Welcome!' he called, 'all is ready for you; we are indeed privileged that this tree is to play such a vital part in your plans.'

Preparations for felling the tree took several days, with at least a hundred people gathering at the site. The evening before it was to come down, a special ceremony of thanksgiving was held. As the light began to fade, the woodland folk advanced with armfuls of flowers to spread them on the ground around the tree and then when night fell they lit hundreds of candles and lamps to illuminate the oak's majestic beauty. It was a truly magical moment, and a reverent silence fell on the assembled multitude.

Then Efflan, in his role of High Priest, stepped forward to lead the prayers for the mighty tree, which so nobly represented the majesty of the Gods' creation.

'The end is the beginning,' he cried, 'this is the way of life. This magnificent tree will now be transformed so that we can complete our task. It is this tree that has made our task possible. We therefore acknowledge and give thanks to the Gods that everything required has been provided. Centuries ago, an acorn was planted and it grew into this mighty oak, before we were even born; this is the wisdom of the Gods. I ask you all now to hold hands and give adoration to this mighty woodland giant. Tomorrow will not be the end, but the beginning of the Gods' almighty plan.'

Everyone then joined hands in the flickering candlelight, and started to sing an ancient chant. Efflan knelt down and bowed before the tree and then all the assembled people did the same.

Next morning, the woodlanders started work digging around the roots of the tree. Merlin, accompanied by Ardel, Brad and Hoel, watched and waited. The local people wanted to contribute to their King and country, so they were happy to do all the work at this stage. They worked long and hard, until, during the afternoon of the following day, the tree began to sway. Then it toppled over with the sound of roots snapping as it fell, and crashed heavily to the ground, which shuddered at the impact.

Ardel then pointed out the exposed roots and branches that would have to be removed. This in itself was a lengthy task. When the trunk had everything stripped from it, the next stage was that it had to be split. This was a daunting prospect, as no one had ever attempted it before with such an enormous tree.

First a large battering-ram was made, together with a frame to carry it. Next, Ardel marked out the places where flint and wooden wedges would be hammered into the side of the tree. This was the real test of his expertise, as one mistake would ruin the timber and all would be lost. Then the pounding of the battering-ram began, with mallets being hit all along the sides of the tree. Very slowly, a fissure started to appear running down the trunk. Ardel directed its path, ensuring it was kept as straight as possible. The fissure widened into a crack, and then a split. Finally, with what sounded almost like a groan, the two halves parted and lay on the ground.

Ardel breathed a sigh of relief and wiped his brow. 'All is well,' he thought, 'my greatest task has been completed.' After this, it would be the turn of Brad and Hoel to start their work on cutting the timber, so it was time for Merlin and Efflan to depart, leaving Ardel in charge.

As Merlin rode along, he felt very happy with the result of this first stage and looked forward to telling King Arthur the news of their successful achievement.

Chapter Twelve

Whittle and Boy wasted no time; they slipped away, under cover of darkness, on their mission to find suitable stones further afield. Making straight across the high plain, they reached the edge of the escarpment and followed it north, in bright moonlight, until they came to the great valley running from east to west.

The descent into the valley proved lengthy and difficult, as the sides were very steep and it was easy to miss your footing at night. Eventually they managed to scramble down; afterwards, it was not long before they came to the river – which, fortunately, the hot summer had reduced to an easily fordable stream – then crossed the rest of the valley floor to begin their walk up the long gradual slope on the other side.

Once out of the valley, Whittle and Boy felt their tired spirits lift.

'Look, Father,' cried Boy, pointing joyfully ahead, 'lots and lots of big stones lying on the ground, just as you remembered!'

'Come on, then,' replied Whittle, 'let's go and see if they're any good to us.'

On arrival, they realised that the stones were visible in such quantities because they had been exposed to the battering of wind and rain for untold centuries. Then the moon disappeared behind a bank of cloud, and they decided it was time they found some shelter for the night.

Fortunately, Whittle remembered the way to the nearest settlement, which lay to their left as he recalled. It was over the next bound, as they looked down, that Boy spotted the glimmer of fires in the distance. On arrival, they found the people were welcoming and friendly, ready to share their food and offer them shelter. Whittle told them of their mission and how they needed to find huge pieces of stone, and lots of it. As they conversed, Whittle and Boy were told there were plenty of stones, known locally as Sarsens. While they ate, the two sat near the fire, a little apart from the others, and talked quietly.

'Things don't look good, Boy,' said Whittle, 'the stone is not uniform in shape, and feels almost as hard as flint. I fear it would be impossible even for Reann to cut!'

'I wish we could do something,' murmured Boy.

'Don't worry, lad,' replied his father, 'we can examine them again tomorrow in daylight; things will look different then.' Whittle thought deeply for a while, eventually saying: 'This is a situation that can only be overcome by time. Tomorrow we must go to the stone field again, sit down there and concentrate, and try to become one with the field. Maybe, somehow, something will be revealed to us.'

Meanwhile, other search parties had been sent out to the south and east on a similar search for suitable stones. Nothing at all had been found in an easterly direction, while to the south, although there was an abundance of stone, it was too soft and so could not be used – Reann would have refused it instantly. One party of searchers had even gone as far as the coast, and found what could be suitable stone there. But ideas of bringing it up-river by raft came to nothing, because the individual stones were so large and heavy that they could not even be lifted onto a raft, let alone carried up such a small river. All attempts to find the right materials seemed to have got nowhere or ended in failure. Everyone was in despair, but no one knew of Whittle and Boy's journey and their determination to find the right stone!

Next morning, after thanking their kind hosts, the two returned to examine the Sarsen stones again in daylight. Whittle sat down among them and was soon lost in thought, while Boy was walking around nearby, roughly measuring the stones.

'The one good thing about this,' Whittle called to him, 'is that these stones are on a slope, and the earth around them could be dug out quite easily. Then, if it was possible for them to be moved, they could be dragged down the hill.'

Boy sat down next to his father and pondered this.

'So,' he said, 'there are two problems: one, the stone is too hard, agreed, Father?'

'Yes,' replied Whittle somewhat despondently.

'Two,' continued Boy, 'the slope at the other side of the valley is far too high and steep?'

'Yes, that's about it,' replied Whittle even more despondently.

'There must be an answer,' declared Boy stubbornly, 'come on, Father, let's have another look at that slope.'

They spent the whole of the next day looking for possible routes up the side of the escarpment onto the high plain, but without success.

'Well, Boy, we have done all we can, and there seems to be no way round the problem,' Whittle eventually had to admit, 'I will have to report back now to the High Council with our findings. They will not be pleased.'

It was when they were starting to walk back as they reached the top of the escarpment that Boy suddenly said 'Father, I feel I must stay here in this place.'

'Very well, you must do as your Spirit tells you,' replied Whittle resignedly. He gave Boy a final hug and they set off in different directions. Whittle reluctantly continued on his depressing homeward journey carrying samples of the Sarsen Stone, while Boy walked alone to the edge of the escarpment, looking out over the great valley and down at the lower levels.

'There must be a way' he thought to himself, 'somewhere out there lies the answer.'

When Whittle returned with his report, he found that the other Chieftains had come back with even more negative results. All had brought samples of the particular stones they had found, however, so it was decided to call a special meeting at which Reann could examine them and give her verdict as to whether or not any were worth further consideration. Two of the Elders were elected to be in charge and all the people who had searched in different locations, Whittle included, were present carrying with them their stone samples. None were aware, however, that Merlin had joined the meeting unannounced and was sitting in the shadows at the back of the hall, listening to all that was said.

When Reann joined them and began to examine the samples carefully one at a time, all present were hoping that she would declare one of them to be suitable. She was very thorough, feeling the stones, tapping them with a hammer, even on one occasion breaking off a piece, all in complete silence. Then she examined all the stones again and eventually rejected all except Whittle's, and stood there with a deep frown on her face.

Then Durrel, the Senior Elder, rose and addressed the meeting, declaring: 'It is clear there is only one type of stone that is strong enough; we will have to take the stone from the north. It will be difficult to shape and cut, but it is by far the best available. There is no choice ... we have no alternative! The choice has been made for us ... once again, we are guided by the Spirit!'

The decision taken, Whittle retraced his steps across the great valley to the place where the Sarsen Stones lay. With him went Reann and a party of hand-picked men from her team of stoneworkers. When they stood on the escarpment at the edge of the valley and looked across, from this vantage point they could just make out the white specks of the Sarsen Stones gleaming in the distance, reflecting the bright sunlight.

On their arrival, Reann almost at once went into a deep, brooding trance-like state, walking ceaselessly up and down, across and back, between the stones. Occasionally she would strike one with a flint hammer. One or two of her companions tried to attract her attention, but others dissuaded them, urging that she should be left alone while she was in such a mood. They knew her of old; it was unwise to disturb her at such times.

The next day, Reann was still brooding; she had risen early in the morning, and they found her cutting a groove in one of the stones, striking the blows furiously with all her might. Then she called to one of the men to assist as she attempted to drill a hole using one of several flint-headed tools she had brought with her. Through all this, Reann remained looking very unhappy. Then, finally, she spoke, muttering to herself, 'You have no idea how difficult it will be … it can be done, but it will not be easy!'

Following this decision, the party of stoneworkers agreed to make camp there and then, while Whittle arranged with the local Chieftain for them to receive regular supplies of food and drink. Whittle then had to return to his home on the high plain; his role where the stones were concerned was ended.

Working together, as always, the stone-working team spent the next few days erecting shelters and setting up a permanent camp. The local people did not need to be told to keep away; those that did want to join in the work approached their Chieftain with honour and respect to ask if they might do so.

The strong ones who were selected had a chance to prove their worth. Many were chosen, but few could sustain the tough conditions. The work was soul-destroying; it involved battling with unforgiving stone and straining with backbreaking toil in all weathers. Such Herculean efforts called for a certain type of individual. Reann herself was an example to all, tireless in her activity and focussed on one thing only, the stone. Slowly, as the days passed, a system began to emerge. It meant that some people would work for one hour and then others would take over, so those who had been handling and cutting the stone could rest. At the same time, Reann was teaching other workers to create and construct levers and other lifting devices. The whole operation was going to be a long, tough haul; they all knew it, yet no one complained.

Back in their village on the high plain, Boy had reappeared and met up with his father again.

Boy spoke first, saying 'You had the right answer, Father. They have started work on the Sarsen Stones.'

'Yes, I left them as they were beginning to build their camp,' Whittle replied, 'I saw it again recently across the valley; it is completed now, so it looks as though they mean to stay. You know, Boy, our next task is to find a route along which the stones can be transported back here. Have you looked at the land to the Northeast?'

'Yes, Father.'

'Is there a possible route in that direction?'

'None. The river gets too deep and the valley is much tighter.'

Whittle sighed deeply and said despairingly, 'the north is blocked because of the valley, while the west side of the high plain is all steep escarpments.' He sat down and shook his head, remarking sadly: 'Things do not look good.'

'But Father,' Boy burst out eagerly, 'there is a solution after all! I have been to the place where they intend to bring the stones here on the high plain, and I have also been to where the stones are now. There is one, and only one, possible route. I have found a gateway in the escarpment to the Southwest. If the trees were cleared away, you would see that there are no obstacles and no incline. It is truly a gateway through which the stones can pass!'

Whittle was silent for a moment, thinking hard. Then he responded 'Yes, I remember the place you speak of. It is a long way round but, as you say, if we follow the bottom of the escarpment until we reach the gateway, then we can take the stones through and across the plain. You know, I don't believe there is anything along the route that could stop us. Well done, Boy! Come on, let's walk the route ourselves to make absolutely certain!'

Chapter Thirteen

While others were busy with their efforts to bring the Sarsen Stones to the Place of the Solstice, Efflan the High Priest was preparing the site in readiness for their arrival. All had to be done according to ancient custom before construction work on the great building could begin. At the very centre of the Sacred Circle, a number of smaller standing stones were already in place; they had been there for a thousand years or even more. Now they had to be removed; Efflan had arranged for this task to be carried out by a special group of Priests, who knew the proper rituals and ceremonies to be used, and where to keep them secure until the great building had been completed.

However, as King Arthur related to Merlin, these were not the only sacred stones to be found on the Isle of Breton.

'Far out to sea in the West,' he explained, 'there is a small island, which is the most mystical place in the Kingdom. It is mainly rock, with sheer cliffs all around, but is covered with a layer of fertile soil and this beautiful place is known as tableland. On this island is another more important stone circle, created over a thousand years ago.'

'I have heard tales of this island,' murmured Merlin, 'it has great power. It is a place where this world and the Otherworld are connected.'

'That has been true until now,' replied the King, 'our project is surely blessed by the Gods; they know these Blue Stones must be brought to the mainland to become part of the great building. Efflan and you, Merlin, will accompany me, for this is a time of great change and your power and Efflan's wisdom will be needed.'

'We will stand together before the Gods,' said Merlin, 'come, we must speak with Efflan; a rider will be sent out to prepare for our arrival at the coast and our journey will begin at once!'

Everyone in the Royal Palace was used to making arrangements for King Arthur's travels, so it did not take long for everything to be made ready for their visit to the island. Durrel and his fellow Elders would, as usual, see to the governing of the country in his absence, together with the High Council and, when necessary, the Chieftains. Fortunately the work on preparations for the great building could continue, so no time would be lost overall.

They rode westwards along age-old trackways; they did not waste any time and travelled through most of the night. When the royal party eventually reached the coast, it was on a fine, warm morning with a clear sky and a sparkling, choppy sea.

As they gazed out across the water at the island, all three felt they were looking at a heaven on earth, a very special place set apart from the rest of the world. A blessed calm filled their minds, and they felt a great sense of pride that they were chosen with honour to set foot on sacred soil.

A large boat, crewed by oarsmen, was moored ready and waiting for them; as they stepped on board and settled themselves, the leading oarsman cast off and the crew began to row steadily towards the island. As they approached, tossed about somewhat by the choppy waves, King Arthur remembered his two previous visits, the only times he had ever been there; both had been national emergencies when he had sought the Gods' aid to avert seemingly inevitable disaster.

Once had been when he was a very young and inexperienced ruler and a brutal foreign Warlord had attacked the country with a view to becoming Emperor. The other, years later, was when a great plague had killed thousands of his subjects and the entire population was in danger of being wiped out. On each occasion the Gods heard his call for help. The foreign invader was killed in battle, and the plague had suddenly vanished from the land.

When they reached the island, the crew beached the boat and held it steady for them to alight, then pushed it out to sea again and rowed a short distance away, where they shipped oars and waited for King Arthur and the others to return. From the rocky foreshore there was only one route up to the tableland above, by way of a steep stone stairway cut into the towering cliff-face.

Up they went, with large numbers of seabirds wheeling and calling about them, King Arthur first, followed more slowly by Efflan and then Merlin bringing up the rear, watching out for the old High Priest in case he stumbled during his ascent. Eventually the top of the stairway was reached, and they climbed gratefully onto the level surface of the tableland. Up here, the air was fresh and cool; they lifted their faces to the pure, strong breeze which felt so refreshing after their efforts. Already the strange power of the island was beginning to work on them; they felt somehow younger, stronger, and empowered by this mystical land.

They walked together to the centre of the island where the age-old stone circle had been built so long ago. Here they stood apart, still and silent, each man looking out in different directions as they felt the waves of power around them increase. Then, when they knew the time to be right, they came together, entered the stone circle and stood at an equal distance apart, facing each other. They made an imposing and striking trio. King Arthur, tall and upright in his robes of red, gold, and royal purple; Efflan, a trifle stooped with age, but still an imposing and venerable figure, in his gleaming white vestments edged with green and gold sacred oak leaves; and Merlin, soberly clad in silken robes of a greyish hue, which swayed around him like smoke when they were caught by the wind.

Now, Efflan the High Priest called upon the Gods. All three raised their arms to the heavens and looked up into the clouds, which had gathered at their approach. The wind was stronger now, too, and their robes billowed and flapped so much, it almost looked as if they were flying.

The King spoke first, saying 'The time has come for a new beginning.'

Efflan followed, chanting 'For a Golden Age of wisdom and knowledge.'

Finally Merlin added 'To be fixed in time by the almighty power of the Gods.'

Then they prayed in unison: 'Let all power of the Gods be directed to our Centre of Excellence, where time revolves and the seasons connect.' There was silence for a moment, then from the sky came a loud rumble of thunder.

The wind increased suddenly to gale force, with a mighty rushing sound. Then the clouds dispersed, the sun shone again, and all was serene and peaceful once more.

'The Gods have spoken,' said Efflan, 'they have blessed our task, and approve that the power of these ancient stones should be transported into our new Centre of Excellence.'

The religious order of Priests, who lived on the island, were told what had occurred, and before their departure King Arthur, Efflan and Merlin made arrangements for the stones to be moved. Following their return to the mainland, this time being rowed across a calm sea, the Priests began their important task. Various rituals and ceremonies would need to be carried out before the stones could even be touched.

Once these had been successfully completed, the Blue Stones were carefully dug up. Each one was placed inside the two split halves of a tree trunk, which were lashed together with strong rope. They were then lowered down the cliffs to the water, where extra ballast was added in the form of large logs strapped onto the outside. The precious cargo was then buoyant enough to be floated to the mainland, where the stones in their wooden casing were rolled up the beach ready to go to their final destination.

Meanwhile, other events connected with the great project were taking place at the same time all over the country. In the territory of the woodland folk, Brad and Hoel continued their work on Merlin's gigantic Stoneroller. They had eventually mastered the plans, and understood how the various wooden pieces fitted together. They started to cut the wood into pieces so that it would fit around a stone, but lengthways; as these pieces would span the full length, they needed to be even longer than the stone itself so they could be fastened together at each end. Then came four sections that would wrap around the stone on either end, and finally another four pieces, which would lock the whole thing together. This meant that the stone would be literally parcelled up inside a wooden casement, all bound together with thick rope.

What was so ingenious about Merlin's design was the fact that the rope only held the wood in position. It was the wood that took all the weight, so in fact the heavier the stone, the tighter it locked together. Self-locking and amazingly strong, the Stoneroller felt "right" to Brad and Hoel, and they believed absolutely that it would work. Once assembled, it would be nearly twice as high as a man and three times as long – it was gigantic in size and it had to be, to carry such massive stones.

Brad and Hoel also knew that, at this early stage, they could delegate most of the work because the wood was still green and unseasoned, so that all the shaped pieces for the Stoneroller only needed to be roughed out initially. To undertake this task, there was no shortage of volunteers; everyone wanted to take part in the King and Merlin's great project. The tools they used were adzes and axes made of bronze, the strongest and sharpest available. Brad and Hoel allowed them to take plenty of time over this work, as the wood needed to season properly. Once roughed out correctly, the pieces would have to be placed on sleds and hauled back across the country, to be finished off closer to the stones.

His task in finding and accurately splitting the great oak tree successfully completed, Ardel had gone further north to select the best timbers for the great building's roof beams. To the north lay the High Mountains, the only area where the tallest and straightest trees could be found in sufficient quantities. Other people were looking for trees with ample girths, which could be used for the huge buttresses that would support the outside of the great building. Other tasks were spread throughout different districts, as most tribes and settlements were eager to contribute. Some had agreed to provide strong ropes and similar essential items of equipment. Others, skilled in basket weaving, were making extra-large ones to be used for transporting huge amounts of soil. In fact, these baskets were so big, that once filled they could not be lifted, only rolled. They were important because there would be more excavations carried out on this project than anything ever before.

Nearer to home, Whittle and Boy had double-checked the route the Sarsen Stones would have to take, and Whittle had marked it out personally. All the settlements in his tribe were busily engaged in removing hundreds of trees, levelling the ground and draining waterlogged areas. He insisted that the path should be very wide, to make the moving of the great stones absolutely obstacle-free, and to allow the men to move about freely and to have all the space they needed to steer the massive roller. This was a major task and it would take many months for the route to be prepared and completed, even though they had a team of strong horses to help pull out all the trees.

Behind the scenes, in a secret location, Merlin was working with Old Sniffy, devising new and more efficient ways to make furnace fires.

'We must achieve temperatures hotter than anything else reached before,' urged Merlin, 'let us experiment with longer tunnels to draw the air, and taller, broader chimneys to vent the smoke.' He went on to talk of mixing things called compounds and heating them together to create new and more powerful substances.

Old Sniffy did not understand most of the theory behind what they were doing, but he was happy because, to his mind, the bigger and hotter the fire, the better.

As they worked, Merlin warned him to keep silent. 'No one must know of these things,' he emphasised strongly, 'you must retain this secret for the rest of your life. What we are achieving here will play a vital part in all our plans; only King Arthur himself is privy to what we are doing.'

The old man was an expert in keeping things to himself. 'Yes, Master Merlin,' he replied. Old Sniffy then smiled to himself; he had spent years keeping things secret, and had no intention of changing the habit of a lifetime.

Little by little, everything was literally starting to come together, with materials being brought in from all over the Kingdom. While all this was going on, however, King Arthur still had to attend to his affairs of state. His Ministers kept him informed daily of progress and this allowed him to keep in regular touch with Merlin. Whenever they could, they spent time together sharing their knowledge and their memories. Merlin would tell the King of the Esoteric, the secrets of alchemy and the sacred arts of geometry and mathematics. For his part, King Arthur would relate events that had happened during his lifetime, involving some of the greatest events in history, and he would also tell Merlin stories from the past, of great battles, fought and won, in times long ago.

Everything seemed to be going well with the great project. Those working on it were happy and inspired; new and progressive ideas were the order of the day.

But in his dark, shuttered room with only his toad for company, Modred was busy with his own diabolical plans. He continued plotting to achieve his ultimate objective, to be lord and master over all and, by now, had wormed his way into the senior ranks of the High Council. Because other members were distracted by the construction of the great building, his evil influence was being allowed to grow all the time by default.

Sensing the weakness of others, he would slyly discredit any who spoke against him while arranging promotions for his own bribed followers. So, quietly and unopposed, Modred was slowly taking over, more and more, without anyone realising. His tentacles of evil were spreading all over the country through a network of lies and deceit, aided by fear and intimidation, better known as Potter and Bullpin with their bands of cut-throats and criminals. It would be only a matter of time before Modred's scheming would result in his having a stranglehold on the country, which, in turn, would lead to disaster or even death.

Chapter Fourteen

The Priests on the island had carried out their appointed task to perfection. All of the ancient Blue Stones had been blessed and then reverently dug out of the ground. The Priests had laboured hard; many of the stones had about a third of their total length buried in the earth, while as much as half of some others had lain hidden from view. They bound each stone in a wooden roller and then lowered them down the cliff, which proved to be a very dangerous undertaking. When, finally, the Blue Stones were on the small section of beach south of the island, extra wood for ballast was attached, and this made a virtual raft for each one to be floated to the mainland. Thanks to their skill, none of the stones were broken; all made the journey intact.

Everything had been done according to Efflan's instructions, as the whole operation had been planned and timed to coincide with the approach of the Summer Solstice.

'From the moment all the Blue Stones reached the mainland,' he told the leaders of those who were given the task of transporting them, 'you have almost a month to get the first stone to the Place of the Summer Solstice by noon on Midsummer Day. This is vital; everything depends on you and your men, and you must not fail!'

He went on to explain, 'This is because the sacred Blue Stones carry within them all the authority and power of the Gods, which will be transferred to our great new Centre. It will take faith and courage, but. when you have succeeded, all will be well for ever and eternity!' Everyone cheered loudly and left to begin their arduous task.

Efflan himself chose the first stone to make the journey, and held a ceremony of consecration over it to protect it from harm. A party of thirty men had been chosen as the appropriate number. Hand-picked, for their strength and stamina, they assembled around the stone, eager to be started on their way.

They pulled and heaved on it in unison, taking the time from their leader, and soon it began to roll along relatively easily. The going was straightforward on level ground, but the numerous ditches and hollows that studded the landscape were soon found to be a major hazard. With these, the stone had to be manhandled across; it was hard and tiring labour that could create hours of delay.

The main fear, however, was the danger posed by heavy rain. Prolonged downpours could result in the whole area being flooded, playing havoc with the timetable. It would be impossible to move the stone if this occurred, and all their plans would be thwarted. To speed their journey, the team leader wanted to use horses for much-needed extra pulling power, but Efflan forbade it.

'This work must be done by human power alone,' he insisted when they made their suggestion, 'the task has been given to us by the Gods, and it must be carried out accordingly.'

The stone was pulled and rolled along throughout each day; their only hope was to work as a team with everyone pulling together. There were few breaks and very little rest, yet they sang as they trudged along their way. People offered to help, but they were told that it was forbidden; this was a challenge given to them and them alone. It took many days and weeks of blood, sweat, toil and pain. A stranger chancing upon the awesome struggle would have called it slavery of the worst kind; those involved called it honour and glory, and undertook it gladly. Suffering was an integral part of the Great Undertaking, borne with great fortitude, but, even so, some fell by the wayside due to fatigue or injury and had to be left behind. As the days passed, everyone continued to give of their best, lustily singing stirring choruses as they pulled and heaved in unison, while the stone moved inexorably ever closer to its destination.

Merlin watched from a distance. Standing on a solitary hill, he marvelled at their stamina.

'From here they look like ants,' he mused to himself, 'tiny creatures incapable of any feats of strength, yet there they are pulling and rolling along a great burden many times heavier than all of them put together. Blest indeed is a land where people freely give of their time and strength to such an extent in serving the common good.'

On the morning before Midsummer Day they reached the gateway which Boy had discovered, and to the loud applause of the crowds which had come to cheer them on, the stone was hauled through the gateway; the last stage had been safely reached. So arduous had the journey been, that six of the men had been lost through injury, but their hearts were high as Midsummer Day dawned and they hauled their burden the last few miles. They knew now, they would fulfil their duty to the Gods, and the power of the Blue Stones would be enshrined at the heart of the new Centre of Excellence.

Meanwhile, at that very place, Efflan had arranged for a great gathering to assemble on the occasion of the Summer Solstice. A wooden platform had been constructed with a ramp leading up to it; this was to mark the celebration of both the Summer Solstice and the arrival of the first sacred Blue Stone. The Elders and other dignitaries were seated at the rear of the platform, so that the chosen speakers could come forward and be seen by everyone when they addressed the people below. Large crowds were always present to celebrate a Solstice, and on this occasion, literally thousands of people had arrived from all over the country, many having travelled for days and even weeks so as to be present at such an important event.

When the time was right, Brenon, as High Chieftain, was the first to speak. He strode forward to the edge of the platform and raised his arms. Everything went quiet.

'Welcome!' he cried, 'we are here today to represent every man, woman and child in the country. We are here to acknowledge a new beginning. Most of you can only guess at what is happening; you have no doubt heard all kinds of mysterious stories. I tell you now, we are building a huge and magnificent Centre, which will stand as the highest symbol of excellence ever to exist. It will be a place of authority and power, where right and good will prevail. Many qualities will be needed to achieve these standards; we must continue as we have begun, working together in unity, co-operation, love and spirituality. It is here that we will create a level of trust and respect that will give honour to all our people. I will now ask the High Priest, Efflan, to speak.'

Efflan came forward and took Brenon's place. A striking figure in his flowing white vestments, he stretched his arms out wide in blessing, and addressed all those below.

'Greetings!' he called out, 'the spirit of the Gods be with you. I am here as the ambassador for the Gods. Around us, as I speak, there are powers beyond our understanding at work. The process of construction has already begun; it started before we were born and will continue long after we die. Their wisdom is beyond the reach of human comprehension, but, even so, we can acknowledge what is happening. Today, we have come together to pray and give thanks to the Gods for what has been, what is now, and what is to come.'

'Behold!' he cried suddenly, pointing dramatically to the West. A horn sounded, to be answered by another one in the distance. All heads turned to see what was happening. Then, over the horizon, silhouetted prominently against the sky, the team of men pulling the first of the Blue Stones slowly came into view. A mighty cheer went up from the assembled multitude and more horns sounded. With this encouragement, the tired team quickened their pace and the stone was soon pulled and rolled into the centre of the great circle. The ropes were cut, the wooden outer shell removed, and the stone was revealed in all its glory.

Efflan shouted aloud: 'The hour appointed by the Gods has come! All their awesome power has now been transferred to this place to mark a new beginning of our great civilization!'

He continued: 'When it is completed, this great building will act as a reflection of the almighty power of the Gods. It will be a place where the Gods can be represented, and where people can come and stand before them. The chosen men and women who take their seats in this Centre will speak with all the authority of the Gods, and their words will be the Law.'

The moment Efflan had finished speaking, King Arthur appeared. Wearing his finest royal ceremonial robes, he walked in procession up the slope and onto the platform with Queen Constance and Princess Guinevere. King Arthur then walked to the front of the platform and stood beside Efflan. He took the wise old High Priest by the hand and raised it into the air. There was a great cheer from the vast crowd, followed by a moment's silence. Then King Arthur began to speak.

'I am your King,' he declared, 'and, as such, I will continue to do everything in my power to protect you and care for you all. It is with honour and pride that I, King

Arthur, do now herald the dawn of a new era, a new time for my people. May the Gods be with you, and as the Sun reaches its zenith, I proclaim a new beginning for us all!'

A shout rang out from the crowd, 'Long live the King!' Then, all the people repeated with one voice: 'Long live the King!' When he had acknowledged this tribute, King Arthur rejoined his Queen and Princess Guinevere.

Seated at the back of the platform, Merlin was watching over the day's events. This, he knew, was a significant moment, a landmark in time, when the powers of the new and the old were joined together in harmony.

'These are good people,' he said to himself, smiling in quiet contemplation, 'if only they knew what lies ahead!'

Chapter Fifteen

With the first of the Blue Stones safely at its destination and the remainder being moved to the site one by one, Merlin's attention switched to the area to the north where the larger Sarsen Stones were being quarried and shaped. Here, Reann and her team were working hard on the two most important of the Trilithons, which were destined to be placed on either side of the Summer Solstice line and topped with a stone lintel. In all, there would be five of these giant three-stone archways, to be set out in the shape of a horseshoe and stand in the middle of the Great Hall.

Reann had been labouring for months on the two biggest stones. The front face of each was curved, while the backs needed to be absolutely flat. Merlin had insisted that the work should be done to perfection, so Reann used all her expertise and she worked to the limit of her capacity.

Finally the first two stones were finished – even lying on the ground they were impressively huge – and were now ready to be transported. Even though Reann had faith in the Stoneroller and understood the principle, she still had doubts.

'Seeing is believing!' she thought to herself. She was not the only one; everyone involved was waiting and trusting that everything would go to plan.

Brad and Hoel had already supervised the wood being roughly shaped; once it had seasoned properly, they were able to carve the pieces into the right size and shape to the best finished precision. Now they were able to set about putting together the different pieces of the Stoneroller. Following Merlin's instructions, they assembled it in sections, with each part designed to fit around a stone so that it would be completely encased in the huge wooden frame.

Lifting the first stone was a herculean task, but everyone rallied round to help; using levers, they were able to lift each end and place it in the cradle, before all the other pieces fitted around it.

Now the huge rectangular stone could be rolled all the way along the side of the escarpment, through the gateway, onto the high plain and to the Place of the Solstice. The fully assembled roller was an awesome sight; once the stone was encased inside and fastened with strong ropes, it measured over twice the height of a man. It was now ready, standing on the hillside, where it was wedged and secured by restraining blocks of wood and stone. The ropes used to haul the Roller were wound around the outside; this gave the men extra pulling power; they now had double their strength using this method.

It was crucial to prevent the Stoneroller from breaking free and careering down the hill at speed. A team of over a hundred and fifty men and women held the restraining ropes, some with stakes set in the ground for added braking power. People were shouting to each other 'Hold still!' There was a feeling of absolute focus with everyone working together.

When they had taken the strain and were poised ready, the blocks in front of the Stoneroller were knocked away. For a moment it remained stationary, with everyone holding on to the ropes for dear life. Then, very gently, they started to lower it slowly down the hill. There was more shouting! After a few false starts and many stops the Stoneroller eventually reached ground level safely.

The orders were given for ropes to be stretched out from the central pivot, or axle points, of the Stoneroller to four teams of strong horses, with eight horses in each team. Once these had been fastened tightly and all the horses were ready, a shout from the leader rang out – 'Forward!' All the drivers urged their steeds onwards, the ropes tautened, and all the men and women heaved on their ropes to help overcome the inertia, then – very slowly at first – the mighty Stoneroller began to move. As it rolled, its own momentum carried it along more rapidly , and the straining horses were able to keep it moving across the undulating countryside.

Whittle and his team were ready to shout and wave instructions, guiding the roller along its chosen path. Up on the high plain, Boy was keeping watch. He had been on the lookout for days to catch his first sight of this mighty device that transported huge stones.

Then, one clear morning, he caught sight of it in the distance and was mesmerised by what he saw. It was a magnificent spectacle, with long lines of men, women and horses, slowly coming into view, pulling behind them a huge revolving giant-sized drum. Everyone who saw the back-breaking efforts being made to roll it along wanted to join in and help, but Whittle, acting as guide and leading scout, forbade it, saying it was too dangerous; they would get in the way and put their lives at risk into the bargain.

Meanwhile, the great juggernaut moved slowly on, taking several hours to move a relatively short distance; this was power on a grand scale.

'That Stoneroller is a mighty object,' thought Boy, 'but it has no feelings; if anyone were to stand in front of it, they would be crushed to death instantly. Where there's power and strength, there's always danger!'

From where he stood, he could see his father directing operations and shouting instructions to the team leaders. He felt an enormous sense of pride as the roller slowly turned and entered the gateway.

When the stone eventually arrived at the site, those transporting it found themselves in the midst of a scene of tremendous activity. Merlin had organised a specialised team of skilled workers, to whom he had explained the layout of the building, and they were busy transforming his instructions into action. The whole site had been marked out with pegs and twine, then, wooden scaffolding had been erected and more ropes and cord stretched out in all directions to ensure the proportions of everything were accurate. The arrival of the first great Sarsen Stone was greeted with shouts of joy, and the wooden Stoneroller was dismantled with great care so that it could be extracted.

This proved to be a very difficult operation because of the heavy weights involved; everyone had to know and understand exactly the right procedures. Once the first stone had been safely removed, the Stoneroller was then reassembled, taken back and made ready for the next stone to be carried. This would be repeated until all the Sarsen Stones had been transported to their final destination.

Huge holes had been dug on either side of the Summer Solstice line for the uprights of the Trilithons. Merlin had planned that these mighty stones should be free-standing in a horseshoe shape in the centre of the Great Hall, so they needed to be set deeply and securely in the ground.

Teams of workers struggled to get them into suitable positions from where they could be raised upright by enormous levers. These were made from specially selected trees, with their bases cut into spade-shaped wedges. Their branches had each been interwoven with willow, transforming them into huge baskets. Then, once the levers had been manoeuvred into position under the stones, the baskets were filled with stone ballast so that they sank down under the weight and in doing so, raised the stone a few inches. It proved a lengthy process, but was very effective in slowly and carefully raising each upright stone into position.

This operation had to be extremely precise, and Merlin insisted on personally measuring the height, distance apart and orientation, to ensure that they were being erected exactly where they should be. Once these measurements had been finalised, the stone uprights were tightly packed with stone wedges, hammered deep into the soil to keep them rigidly in place.

With the Trilithons safely in position, it was then the turn of the thirty stone uprights, which formed the Great Sarsen Circle, to be erected. Once more, the positioning of each was critical, because they would form an integral ring with their lintels locked to them and to each other by mortise and tenon and tongue and groove joints. But that would come later. For the present, their orientation to North and the Summer Solstice line was the vital thing to ensure, so, once again, Merlin had insisted on checking all measurements and calculations himself.

While the great Trilithons had been buried very deeply in the ground, many of the stones in the Sarsen Circle only required very shallow holes. This was because, eventually, they would be safely supported from the outside by huge buttresses.

Meanwhile, to ensure they stayed upright, large amounts of soil were packed around them. This soil had been dug out from an area a considerable distance away from the site, and was transported there in very large baskets. These were rolled up the gradual slope and then emptied on arrival. It was a very lengthy job but eventually, after a whole year had gone by, it was finished and the entire site was a huge mountain of soil. Only the tops of the Great Sarsen Circle stones were visible; sticking out, as were the tops of the huge Trilithons, ready now for their lintels to be hauled into place.

Merlin was pleased his Stoneroller had transported every stone to the site, and despite his own secret doubts at times, neither it, nor a single stone, had been damaged. The whole operation, lengthy though it had been, had proved to be a triumphant success.

'Thank goodness, too,' thought Merlin, 'despite the dangers involved in moving such vast weights, there have been no fatalities. All the men and women involved in the work were conscious of the danger of the operation, with each worker knowing his or her place in the team. The teamwork has been essential, and all has gone according to plan with not a stone out of place.'

Chapter Sixteen

With the uprights of the Sarsen Stones all now in place, it was time for Reann and half her team to leave the quarrying and return to the Place of the Solstice so that they could start work on fitting the stone lintels. Thanks to the great mound of earth that had engulfed the site, this task was made considerably easier than it would otherwise have been, as the lintels could be brought to the tops of the upright stones without the need for lifting them up to this height.

First to be tackled was the central horseshoe of Trilithons; the biggest lintel required here being estimated to weigh in excess of ten tons. The task of cutting and dressing these lintels proved the supreme test of Reann's unique skills; this was because they were designed not just to be laid across the uprights, but were carved with mortise and tenon joints so that they fitted snugly and safely onto them.

Then, all thirty lintels required for the Sarsen Circle had to be not only prepared, but tried and tested, by being lifted up and replaced several times to ensure a perfect fit. Reann worked with all the expertise she could muster, and the result was a triumph for her as not a single one failed to fit exactly onto its uprights.

When the last lintel had been lowered securely into place, it was the first time anyone had seen a momentary smile flicker across her normally impassive face.

Everything was done in accordance with Merlin's measurements. He had stressed it was essential that the Sarsen Circle had to measure one hundred feet precisely, as the foot was the unit of length that he had used in all his calculations.

King Arthur and he had decreed that this basic measurement was to become the new standard unit for people to use all over the country. The great building was to set the standard of excellence in all things; length, angle of degree and time itself would also be measured and calibrated.

With the uprights now locked together by their lintels, the time had come to begin constructing the biggest roof ever attempted. As this was to be made entirely of wood, Brad was put in charge of the work. The roof had been designed in such a way that each stone lintel would carry one wooden beam, long enough to reach right up to the apex, where all the beams would meet. To these would be added all the cross members and the roof covering itself.

The uniquely amazing part of this design was the fact that there were to be no wooden internal supports; the Sarsen Circle alone would bear the whole weight of the roof. This Stone Circle in turn would be supported from the outside by thirty huge buttresses, designed to transmit all the weight of the roof directly into the ground. The buttresses, in turn, would be locked into stone footings set in the ground surrounding the building. The whole powerful structure had been designed so that it would literally lock itself together by using the force of gravity.

While Brad was in overall charge of roof construction, his brother Hoel had been chosen to lead the strongest team of workers – 'The Seven Brothers' they called themselves. Their job was to drag the huge logs, that formed the buttresses, over the side of the vast mound of earth and then slide them into place.

All was going smoothly until one day, whilst one of the buttresses was sliding into position, tragedy struck. Suddenly one of the restraining ropes snapped; the buttress, weighing over a ton, careered out of control. There was nothing to stop it, and at that point, Hoel was standing with his back to it, completely unaware anything was amiss. Several people shouted warnings, but it was too late and before anyone could move, Hoel took the full force of the bone-crushing log and was knocked flat. It came to a halt lying across his body, and for a few seconds, there was a stunned silence. Then, the tall, burly figure of Magnus the Norseman raced over and, using all his great strength, managed to lift the log sufficiently for others to drag Hoel clear. But it was too late. Every effort was to no avail; Hoel had died instantly. All work stopped as Brad, who had heard the shouts and raced to the scene, knelt, weeping in a paroxysm of grief and cradled his brother's crushed and broken body.

The next day, Hoel's wife, Megan, and his children were told, then his burial was arranged. His whole family, including his mother and father, were present, together with a large gathering of his friends and fellow workers, who had come to pay their respects and to support Brad, who stood motionless throughout, his face a mask, frozen in grief.

As a mark of the great regard in which Hoel had been held by all, Efflan, as High Priest, conducted the ceremony in person and spoke his epitaph.

'Hoel was a very talented man, gifted in the art of wood,' he began, while everyone nodded in agreement, 'he was also a good husband and father, and we should not forget that he was also a son. Hoel died doing the work that he loved. He will be missed and not forgotten, for, without him, we would not have come this far. I now ask Megan, his wife, to come forward, please, and speak.'

Megan tried to compose herself, embraced her children and began, hesitantly at first: 'This is a moment of great honour for Hoel and his family,' she declared, 'he was my husband and the father of my children. I will miss him more than I can say, but I ask you all not to grieve, for there is no better way to die than in the service of the Gods. I know that Hoel truly believed in the work he was doing and I am certain he has been chosen to become part of that great project which the High Priest assures us will last forever. I therefore ask you all to rejoice and salute the man I truly loved.' Hoel's body was then buried, under the huge stone which supported the buttress that killed him.

It was after Hoel's death that things changed. Before, everyone had worked fast, in a spirit of urgency and haste. Now, that urgency had gone. The working pace from then on became slower and more methodical. Hoel's absence left a large gap in the group; his skill and good company were much missed. Helpful assistance, however, was at hand.

For a long time now, Boy had been eager to join the group and eventually, realising he had grown stronger and more mature, Whittle gave his permission. He lacked any specialised skills, but was able to make himself generally useful, with tasks like carrying water and refreshments to the workers, freeing them to give more time to their tasks, without distractions. It was not long before he had become an accepted member of the group, and soon it was taken for granted, that if anyone wanted anything, they just had to call and Boy would be there.

Even though he was kept busy, running to and fro on errands, Boy, with his keen intelligence, did not miss a thing. He watched the Elders and the Masters, who were supervising the various tasks, and whenever Merlin appeared, he saw how they interacted together, deferring to his superior wisdom. Merlin would bring along armfuls of plans and diagrams and lay them out on a table, while the others gathered round to study and discuss them for hours.

One day, there was a Royal visit; when King Arthur arrived, he wanted to know all about how the work was going and the rate of progress being made on the building construction. As soon as he had greeted Merlin and the group around him, his first question was 'Is everything going according to plan?'

'Yes, Your Majesty,' replied the Chief Foreman, 'all is as it should be; there have been no unexpected hitches or delays, we are right on schedule and there is nothing out of place.'

'Good,' the King responded, 'do you lack any manpower or materials?'

'Thankfully, no, Your Majesty; we have the best team of skilled workers in the country, and all the materials we need at present are on site, while further supplies are already on their way to us here.'

While appearing to busy himself with a number of jobs, Boy was actually listening intently to the conversation and taking everything in. Already he had a good overview of how the construction work was proceeding, and with his keen intelligence, could see how each particular task fitted in precisely with the others. His admiration for Merlin grew with each new thing he learned.

Having satisfied himself that everything was going smoothly according to plan, King Arthur drew Merlin to one side and said quietly to him, 'Unfortunately I am becoming much more involved in affairs of state; for some reason the Elders and the High Council do not seem to be giving their wholehearted attention to matters. There is something distracting them, which is frequently making them unsure how to proceed; they seem to be arguing more among themselves, and the result is that the running of the country is not being carried out efficiently.

'I do not yet know what is amiss, but I desperately need to discover the cause, before real trouble affects the realm. This means, my friend, that from now on, I will not be able to keep in as close contact with you as I would like.'

'Be easy in your mind, my Lord, where this great work is concerned,' replied Merlin reassuringly, 'I shall be entirely focused on matters here for at least another year, or even more. I know the men well now, and I know they are completely dedicated to seeing the project through. Be assured, King Arthur, I and all the others here, will work unceasingly in your absence.'

'My thanks, Merlin,' smiled the King, I know I can depend on you utterly. Now, though,' he added sadly, 'I fear I must depart. Remember, you can call on me for assistance at any time; I will always be available if you should need me.'

'Thank you, also, Your Majesty,' said Merlin, reaching out and taking the King's hand, 'fear not, Arthur, my King but foremost my friend, everything here is going to plan.'

As he watched the King's reluctant departure, Merlin murmured unhappily to himself, 'Everything here may be going to plan, but, like Arthur, I fear all is not well in the country as a whole. I, too, can feel that something is amiss at the centre of things, and I have a sense of foreboding that dark forces may be at work. I wish Arthur well, but somehow I fear for him. However, it is not my ordained task to play a part in ruling the country; the Gods have decreed that my duty lies here.' Then he rejoined the group around the table and once more became immersed in their discussions regarding the plans.

Chapter Seventeen

After Hoel's death, Brad felt very alone. They had been very close, even for brothers, and had often found, that at any given moment, their thoughts were running along the same lines. This made his feelings of isolation and loss very acute, but, somehow, he found the strength to go on and, with a sense of relief, he began to busy himself, once again, with his work on the roof. It came easily to him, and soon began to give him back a sense of purpose and meaning to his life.

By now, the main beams, thirty in total, had all been fixed into position, and all the cross members were also in place. The building was so big, and the roof was so high, that this construction work would have been infinitely more difficult were it not for the soil which was still heaped up inside. This had been a master-stroke of Merlin's foresight; it protected anyone who missed their footing and fell from being injured, and the workers could easily adjust their platforms and workstations to whatever position was required.

Soon, it was time for the roof covering to be applied. Exactly as in the scale replica, Merlin's gift to Princess Guinevere, the roof was made with thousands of triangular wooden tiles. Every tile had a protective coating of beeswax and they all overlapped each other, making it completely waterproof. They were also designed to be interlocking, so the roof could withstand the strongest gales.

Once completed, the roof appeared visually huge. This was, in part, because it extended out beyond the Sarsen Circle and reached all the way down to the ground in places, making the entire structure look bigger than ever. From a birds-eye view, it had the shape of a ten-pointed star, with only the points touching the ground. The effect was both awe-inspiring and extremely beautiful; some of the people likened it to a giant flower placed upside down. At the apex of the roof was a large aperture, which Merlin had designed, allowing direct light to reach virtually every part of the interior. To make it brighter still, the whole of the inside of the roof had been painted white so that it would act as a huge reflector of sunlight. This ensured that, at certain times of day, the interior of the building would be ablaze with light, reflecting into the centre of the Great Hall.

When the last tile was safely in place and Merlin declared that the roof was finished, the entire workforce joined in to help remove the mound of soil that filled the interior. There was a great eagerness, on the part of all concerned, to finish this task as quickly as possible, because everyone was eager to see how the Great Hall would look, once the soil had all been cleared away.

The same giant-sized baskets, in which the earth had been brought to the site, were used again, to take it away. When filled, each one in turn was rolled out of the building and over the edge of the gradual slope. Every time one was sent on its way, a great cheer went up as it rolled all the way down to the bottom of the hill. After working so hard for so long, people greatly enjoyed the relief of seeing something move without having to exhaust themselves. The whole job of clearing out the soil was tackled so energetically that it was completed within a month.

With the Great Hall empty of soil, it could now be seen in all its majesty, the great Trilithons standing like pillars of strength in the centre. All who entered were amazed at the size and wonder of it all. Even the ceiling looked different, with the angle of it appearing very shallow in a graceful arc. It did not seem possible that such a vast and airy structure, larger than anyone had ever seen before, could actually exist, and yet it was solid and real enough. By far the most impressive feature was the blaze of light that shone down from the open apex and bathed the entire Great Hall in its warm glow. So strong was the impact of this, that it produced feelings of wonder, excitement and anticipation in

180

all who entered. The total effect was quite simply breathtaking.

At this stage, Merlin judged the time was right to make an announcement. He called everyone together, and all the workers assembled in the middle of the Great Hall. When everyone was present, he addressed them, saying, 'You have all worked so well, I propose that, in a week's time, we gather here to celebrate in this great new building. This will be especially for you, so bring all your families and friends; you are all welcome, so come along and enjoy yourselves and have a good time!' Everyone then applauded and cheered, before leaving to spread the good news.

A few days before the party, Merlin went to visit Princess Guinevere at the Palace. When he was announced she ran to greet him and led him by the hand into her apartment, all the while saying how much she loved her beautiful house. They discussed it for a few minutes, then Merlin said, 'I have not seen your father, the King, how is he?'

'He has gone on his travels once more,' frowned Guinevere, 'I do not like it when he is away so often, but duty seems to call him from us more and more these days. This time he has gone away to the North, and I do not know when he will return.'

Merlin then asked 'What news of your mother, the Queen, is she in good spirits?'

'Oh, yes!' smiled Guinevere, 'she has decided to prepare a new set of apartments for when my father returns, and as usual, she is keeping busy, supervising every detail of the decorations and furnishings.'

'Good,' said Merlin, 'and how about you, my dear, apart from missing your father, is all well with you?'

The Princess hesitated, then replied 'Well, you know I love the house you made for me, and I love all my friends. It's just that, well – something is missing!'

'I know exactly what you mean,' Merlin replied reassuringly. 'Look, I have an idea,' he went on, 'how would you like to accompany me to a party?'

Guinevere hesitated again, then said apologetically, 'Oh! You are very kind, Merlin, but I really have been to so many parties!'

'That, I know,' responded Merlin, 'but this time I don't want to invite a royal Princess, I want to invite you!'

'Whatever do you mean?' asked Guinevere, very puzzled by this.

'You can go as someone else, a peasant girl, perhaps. Go incognito, lose your royal identity for a night, and have some carefree fun just like other people! No one will know, except me. Wouldn't you enjoy that?'

The Princess thought for a moment. She was somewhat taken aback, and, for an instant, she was on the verge of politely refusing. Then a flash of joy came to her: to be free for a whole evening with no protocol or etiquette! Laughing, she turned to Merlin and held out her arms to him.

'You are a mind reader, dear Merlin,' she burst out, 'you always know what's best for me. Yes, yes, a peasant girl will come to your party, and she will have a lovely time. Thank you so much, Merlin; for once, my real self is going to have some fun!'

The day of the eagerly awaited celebration party eventually arrived, and everyone gathered, once again, inside the Great Hall, all wearing their best clothes and looking forward to a wonderful evening. Those who had not seen inside the Great Hall before looked around them in awed amazement. It was so vast, and so majestic. That evening it looked beautiful, too, decorated with flowers everywhere and illuminated with hundreds of flickering candles. The central space had been kept clear and was surrounded by tables, set out with plenty of food and drink for all, while seating had thoughtfully been provided for the more elderly folk.

When the celebrations started, the musicians struck up a merry tune and there was a great deal of singing and dancing, while the small children were kept amused with party games.

Boy had invited his father Whittle, together with his mother and sister. They all joined in the dancing, holding hands and spinning round in circles. His exertions made Boy go as red in the face as though he was blushing; the music was so lively, it set people prancing about and getting giddy with excitement.

It was as Boy was jigging around and dancing backwards and forwards that he suddenly noticed a beautiful young girl. She wore a plain brown dress, with no jewellery, and had her hair concealed under a small cap, but her poise and beauty of features marked her out in Boy's eyes as very special. When he first saw her, she was standing quietly, by herself, among the onlookers, watching the dancing with a rather wistful expression.

'Who is she,' he thought, 'and where is she from?'

By now, his eyes were fixed firmly on her; he was convinced he was looking at the loveliest girl in the world. He was determined to speak to her, and wondered how best to get closer.

When the music stopped and the dancers, all out of breath, came to a sudden halt, Boy had his chance. Realising it was now or never, he moved across to where the beautiful girl was watching the merrymaking and stood beside her. Then, blushing furiously, he smiled at her. To his amazement, she smiled back.

'Hello,' said Boy.

'Who are you?' she replied.

Her voice was soft and musical, and sent shivers down Boy's spine.

'My name is Boy,' he told her proudly, 'I am the son of a Chieftain.'

Intrigued, she asked, 'Is that your real name?'

'Yes, that's what I'm known as.'

'Well,' she laughed, 'my name is Grainne'.

Boy nervously blushed and replied, 'I am very pleased to meet you; are you here with your family?'

The girl, who called herself Grainne, hesitated for a moment. 'Er, no. A friend invited me.'

All this time Boy had been frantically plucking up his courage, and now blurted out 'W-would you like to dance with me?'

The next few seconds seemed like an eternity, then to his amazement and delight, the beautiful girl replied, 'Why, yes, thank you; I should love to!' She definitely liked the look of this tall, handsome boy with his dark hair and broad shoulders, and wanted to spend more time with him.

As he led her into the next dance, Boy felt he was walking on air, the luckiest person alive! 'Now,' he

185

thought, 'I mustn't be clumsy and tread on her toes; I must be very careful.'

But when they began to dance all his shyness melted away. She was a beautiful dancer, moving in time to the music with him, so they seemed like one being. As they danced, he first held her hand, then in the more energetic parts, greatly daring, he put his arm around her. Momentarily she flinched, and then flashed him a dazzling smile as they carried on dancing.

The pace grew more energetic as the dance progressed, and suddenly Grainne's cap flew off into the crowd, releasing a glorious cascade of long red-gold hair. For an instant Boy's memory told him he had seen something like it before, but they didn't stop dancing for a moment, and as far as he was concerned he wanted the evening to go on for ever!

In another part of the Hall, Whittle was dancing with his wife Jenny; seeing Boy with his unexpected partner he nudged her and pointed them out, laughing with joy at his son's good fortune. His big blond friend from the north, Magnus, usually the strong silent type, had also earlier managed to find himself a partner, so Whittle was overjoyed to see that a good time was being had by all. Even Merlin was dancing with a group, in a somewhat slow and stately fashion, happy to join in the fun and laughter.

The party was a great success; it proved a wonderful occasion when everybody had a good time, and it went on until darkness fell. Then, Merlin called a halt to the dancing, and asked all the guests to take and light a candle. They did so, and crowded into the centre of the Great Hall, holding the candles to illuminate their faces. Everyone looked at each other, Boy with his eyes locked with those of the lovely Grainne; all around was a sea of smiling faces. They could not have been happier; even the simplest among them could feel the spirituality.

Then Merlin spoke, his words dropping clearly into the silence, 'We are here, this evening, at the first gathering ever to be held in this Great Hall. You are beautiful people; give peace and love to each other and remember this day; for me it has been one of the happiest days of my life. Will you all now take a drink, and I will give you a toast! Raise your cups, as I name this Great Hall – Stonehenge!' Everyone cheered and shouted 'Stonehenge!' The sound reverberated around the Great Hall.

By this time, the candles were guttering and going out one by one. Boy suddenly realised that Grainne was no longer beside him. He looked frantically around, and caught a glimpse of her for an instant in the last glimmer of light moving through the crowd, then she was gone.

Quickly he began to search, high and low, to try and locate her, but, by now, it was too dark.

Afterwards, he walked home in a happy daze, dreaming of Grainne. He had met and danced with the most beautiful girl in the world!

Chapter Eighteen

The party had been a great success; people were so relaxed and in holiday mood afterwards, that Merlin thought it wise to allow all the work teams a few weeks break, before starting on the next stage of construction. This was to make and lay the main floor, and when work started again, everyone involved set to with renewed vigour.

The floor was constructed entirely of wood, cut into large, heavy sections, one foot thick, all supported from underneath by heavy stone slabs. These tapered lengths of timber ran from the centre of the Great Hall to the outside, radiating out like a huge circular fan. All the pieces were fitted together with tongue and groove joints, so that as each piece slid into position, it locked the whole floor tightly together.

Also, while the floor was being laid, holes were dug and the Blue Stones were positioned exactly to Merlin's instructions. In fact, he insisted on being there, because it was these Blue Stones that would carry all the power to the great seats from which the law would be administered.

Once the floor was in place, the task of cutting, scraping and polishing it to perfection began. Inset into the centre of the floor was a large symbol, based on the plan of the building. Measuring five feet across, it was made of polished granite – which looked like marble – inlaid with pure gold, and took the shape of a ten-pointed star, exactly echoing the outline of the Great Hall as seen from above. This provided a constant reminder to all that it was Stonehenge itself which was held in reverence!

When all this had been completed to Merlin's exacting standards, the walls and doors were fitted around the perimeter of the floor. Merlin had designed everything to be both mysterious and beguiling; for example, if people did not know where the doors had been positioned they were unable to find them. It truly was a wonder to behold, and now the vast building was nearly complete; all that remained was to solve the problem posed by the open aperture at the apex, because while it allowed light to flood the interior, it also permitted rain to penetrate inside. This meant that each time it rained, covers had to be placed over the top, making it too dark to work and so delaying the schedule.

Fortunately, during most of the construction, the weather remained fine, and people were able to work throughout the hours of daylight. One day, however, the progress of the work schedule was rudely interrupted by the unannounced arrival of Modred, accompanied by his henchmen, Potter and Bullpin, with their band of morons.

The men who had been posted around the building to keep out unwanted visitors were roughly pushed aside, and Modred just forced his way in, acting as if the Great Hall was his private property. When his sinister black-clad form, along with his escort, were seen advancing, everyone left their work and huddled fearfully back into the safety of the shadows; all knew it was very unwise to attract the attention of Modred or his band of evil followers.

Boy happened to be working on the roof near the apex when they entered, and as he looked down, he shivered as he saw the black figures moving to and fro, far below him.

'Ugh!' he thought to himself in disgust, 'they look just like a lot of cockroaches scuttling about down there! I wonder why they've come here; they certainly aren't welcome.'

In fact, Modred was determined to see for himself if the building bore any resemblance to the glowing reports he had heard. What he found himself looking at astonished and delighted him; this vast Great Hall would be ideal for his own evil purposes.

'Aha!' he thought to himself, 'this is the perfect place, everyone can come here and worship me! It might have been built for me; I must and shall have it before anyone else. The time has come to bring all my plotting and scheming to fruition, so I can take action to ensure it becomes mine and mine alone – the perfect setting for my Lord and Master, Cernunnos! All will bow in homage, as he manifests himself in me!'

He threw back his head and laughed, a sinister high-pitched sound which made people's blood run cold, then, suddenly, he turned on his heel without a word and, followed by his entourage, he swept out of the building in a frenzy, like a man driven by demons.

Everyone breathed a great sigh of relief when he had gone; it was as if a dark shadow had been lifted from their hearts and minds, and it took some time before, eventually, things returned to normal.

Merlin had not been present to witness Modred's unwelcome visit. With construction of Stonehenge so far advanced, he had been spending more time with Old Sniffy working on the development of ever-hotter furnaces, which were situated about four miles away, hidden deep in the woods. Old Sniffy had managed to recruit a number of other expert smelters and he was keeping them all busy, but had sited them well away from each other in different parts of the forest so that none of the group could gossip and exchange information. Old Sniffy was a past master at keeping his professional secrets to himself, and for this project he had arranged matters so that only he was fully aware of what was being achieved.

It was at this time that Merlin also took the decision to involve Brad in their secret plans. On the next day after Modred's visit, he persuaded Old Sniffy to accompany him to Stonehenge and meet Brad in person, so that he could explain fully what was expected of him. Normally he would not have dragged Old Sniffy away from his beloved fires, but the latter's admiration and respect for Merlin was now such that he would have followed him anywhere – 'even down into the Otherworld if needs be', he would say, with a rare cackle of laughter.

Just before they arrived, Boy was, as usual, busily sweeping and doing odd jobs when his curiosity was aroused as he saw Merlin disappearing round a corner of the huge Trilithons accompanied by a wizened, gnarled old figure, a man he had not seen before.

Then Merlin reappeared, called Brad from his work, took him by the arm as they greeted each other and then disappeared once more. When Merlin, Old Sniffy and Brad were closeted together behind the Main Trilithon, Boy was listening intently and realised he was being made privy to the most astounding secret information he had ever heard. His naturally inquisitive impulses were now fully alerted, he skilfully managed to appear involved in his work, while gradually edging closer to where he had last seen them.

Peering round the corner, Boy could just see them in the shadows and heard a murmur of voices. Greatly daring, half in fear of Merlin's wrath if he was caught, he sidled closer and closer until, if he listened hard enough, he could hear what they were saying. To his surprise, Merlin was asking Brad to work on the apex alone, and to swear not to let anyone else know about the work they would entrust to him.

Boy had somehow suspected that Merlin had something extra-special planned for Stonehenge and that it must be going to happen soon, as construction was already far advanced and very near to completion. He started to ponder; 'What has Merlin got in mind?' he thought, 'although the great seats have not yet been fitted, and the apex remains unfinished, the remainder of Stonehenge is ready for King Arthur to see when he returns from his visit to the North.' Boy had also grown physically and mentally over the last few years, and now possessed the strength and skill to work alongside the best woodworkers, but his curiosity always got the better of him. His mind raced ahead into the future, as he tried to imagine how Stonehenge would look when finally completed.

The voices had sunk to a low whisper and then fallen silent, so Boy had ceased trying to listen and turned again to his work in earnest. His mind was still racing and he was in a dreamlike state when he was startled to hear a sudden voice behind him, saying 'Well, young man!' Boy turned quickly; Merlin stood there, looking rather stern.

'Oh, hello, Sir.' he stammered, embarrassed to be confronted by such an important person.

Merlin continued, 'I gather from your presence that there is not much you don't know about Stonehenge?'

Boy replied, 'Oh dear, I am sorry if I overheard you; I didn't mean to spy, I was just curious as to what will happen next.'

'Very good,' said Merlin, looking less stern now, 'I know of your curiosity, and I also know you have a keen mind.' Merlin then asked him, 'As you already know so much, would you like to know more?'

'Oh, yes please!' said Boy eagerly, 'I certainly would!'

'I thought so,' Merlin smiled, 'in that case, come with me and you will learn!'

They walked across the floor and into the centre of the Great Hall, where all Merlin's working drawings and plans were set out on tables. Merlin showed each one to Boy, in turn, explaining the sacred measurements and mathematics that had been used in the construction of the building. He laid particular stress on what the structure was to be used for, and most importantly, how it worked in relation to the sun.

Boy was absolutely dumbstruck. There was so much to understand and take in; he had no idea that it had been so elaborately planned, and the reasoning behind it all was far beyond anything he could have imagined. He felt that pictures were being opened in his mind stretching away to limitless horizons. The best-kept secret was the apex; no one would ever know, because it was too high and people would never be able to work it out.

Somewhat dazed, bewildered and absolutely enthralled by what he was being told, Boy asked Merlin, 'W-why are you telling me this? – I'm no expert, only an inexperienced worker.'

'Yes, you are indeed young and inexperienced,' he replied, 'but you have an agile mind, great curiosity and a willingness to learn. I did not choose you, you were here already, and possibly it was destiny that brought you here. So, I must, and will, teach you all I know about Stonehenge.'

From that day onwards, Boy listened, enthralled, to Merlin's wisdom. He was an excellent pupil, not least because his father had taught him that the best way to learn was to listen.

'How suddenly my life has changed,' he thought, 'from sweeping the floor to Merlin's pupil in a single day! I wonder what else the future has in store for me?'

Chapter Nineteen

Princess Guinevere had woken early. For a moment, still half asleep, she wondered why, then quickly remembered that this was a very special day.

'Hurray,' she cried aloud, 'my Father's coming home today!'

She jumped out of bed and ran barefooted to where she could see the sun, which was already beginning to shine.

'Perfect,' she thought, 'it's going to be a lovely, fine day, so I can wear my best clothes. I hope he likes my new long dress; oh, I've got so much to tell him after all this time!'

When her young maid arrived to prepare her for the occasion, she found the Princess dancing happily around the room out of sheer joy at the prospect of her father's return.

Queen Constance was determined that her husband's return from his prolonged Royal Tour should be celebrated in proper style. She had ordered that lookouts should be posted, at intervals, for many miles along the track-way so that word could be sent at the first sign of the King's approach. Everything had been made ready; outside the Palace, flowers had been strewn lavishly, so that they formed a thick carpet on the approach to the main gates.

Inside, the Queen had ensured that their new apartments were ready, while food, drink and music had been prepared to greet her beloved husband. She stood on the threshold, regally attired, with Guinevere beside her, looking very beautiful and grown-up in her new dress, both radiantly happy and eagerly awaiting King Arthur's arrival.

After what seemed like ages, word came that the Royal party was approaching. When they finally arrived, smiling and waving to acknowledge the shouts of welcome from the large crowds that had gathered, the party halted and the head of the King's escort knocked three times with his ceremonial staff on the front gates of the Palace. They immediately opened and the King entered, amid loud cheering. The entire Royal household was there to greet him, and he paused briefly to acknowledge them all.

Then he hastened to the new Royal apartments, where he found the doors open and his lovely wife and daughter waiting to welcome him. He opened his arms, cried a greeting, and the two people he loved most in all the world rushed into his embrace.

The celebrations to mark King Arthur's homecoming lasted for a whole week; Queen Constance was determined that he should have time to rest and fully recover from his long and arduous Tour. The royal family were together again, and they all three wanted to make the most of this precious time.

King Arthur was eager to hear of everything that had occurred during his absence, and particularly how the building of Stonehenge was progressing. Merlin had been sending him regular reports, but some had failed to reach him, so he was keen to learn how far the project had actually advanced. When a week had passed, he felt ready and eager to view the great building for himself; he wanted time and space to really get the feel of the place and absorb its atmosphere.

The day was fixed for King Arthur's first visit to Stonehenge. Durrel, the Senior Elder, arranged that no royal duties should be transacted on that day, and that no one else would be in the building except Merlin and King Arthur. When the King saw the huge size and shape of Stonehenge on the horizon, he was struck with amazement at the sheer power of the magnificent building. Guinevere's miniature house had been transformed into something truly awe-inspiring and magnificent, the like of which had never existed before. Merlin, who was standing at the main door to greet his royal friend, smiled when he saw the effect the exterior of Stonehenge was having.

'Welcome, Your Majesty,' he said proudly, 'please enter; all is ready for your Royal approval.'

King Arthur strode inside, then halted and looked around him in amazement; he was absolutely astounded at what he saw, all clearly illuminated by the great beam of light that blazed down from the open apex.

'Merlin,' he exclaimed in awe-struck tones, 'I had no idea... this – this is beyond words!'

Merlin, still smiling, said nothing, but let the King walk around and explore the vast interior further. Whilst they walked and talked, the King became aware of his own voice. He could hear every sound with absolute clarity.

Puzzled, he asked 'What is it, Merlin, as I speak?'

'Ah, Sire,' explained Merlin, 'this Great Hall has been designed to have perfect acoustics, which means that when you speak, the sound can be heard in every part, without you having to raise your voice.'

Suddenly the King started to laugh, with a mixture of joy and relief, saying 'It's absolutely wonderful; Merlin, you are a genius!'

Merlin bowed in acknowledgement and motioned King Arthur to accompany him. They proceeded slowly all the way around the interior while Merlin described how the building would work, pointing out all the special features and revealing all its hidden secrets.

'Here in the centre of the Great Hall,' he explained, 'I propose to place a Round Table where, on occasions of high ceremony and feast days, the highest and most important personages in the land will be seated. The table will be round, so that no one person can be at the head, because we acknowledge that the Gods are at its centre.'

Finally, the King could contain himself no longer and burst out 'Merlin, there is not one thing missing, you have thought of everything!'

'In fact, Sire,' he replied, 'there are still one or two finishing touches to be put in place. I can promise you even more surprises, but yes, overall we are here to witness or glimpse the perfection of what is possible.'

Then, the superbly gleaming wooden floor caught the King's eye, with its dramatic star-shaped symbol, inlaid with gold, echoing the overall shape of Stonehenge.

'It is a wonderfully intricate pattern,' he said admiringly, 'absolutely astounding.'

'Yes, Your Majesty,' replied Merlin, 'it is a symbol of life itself.'

As he talked, Merlin found he had walked ahead of the King, who had once again stopped to wonder at the intricacy of the symbol's inlay and its superb craftsmanship. Turning, the old man gave a sharp intake of breath. Standing in the centre of the symbol, Arthur was bathed from head to foot in the bright golden light that shone down from the apex like a spotlight.

For a moment, Merlin thought he had seen a vision; the King gleamed like an apparition not of this world, as though transported into Stonehenge and transformed into an angel of light. An instant later, Arthur stepped towards Merlin out of the brightness, and the spell was broken. But it had unnerved Merlin; his inner eye had, for an instant, glimpsed the King as a figure that was not a living being, and it had reinforced his sense of foreboding concerning the future.

Then, Merlin focused back on the present and recalled that there was yet one more marvel to present to King Arthur while they were alone, and, banishing his unease, he moved over to a wooden stand, on which something lay covered with a richly woven cloth.

'Now, Sire,' he said, 'to mark the occasion of your first visit to Stonehenge, I have a gift for you.'

Deftly removing the cloth, he revealed a magnificent sword. The hilt of the weapon was covered with gold leaf, while the pommel had a large jewel set in it, cut and faceted like the star-shaped pattern on the floor. The scabbard, too, was adorned with gold leaf, chased in a design of intertwining threads of silver and gold, inlaid with precious gems.

For a moment, King Arthur was speechless at the sight of so rich and rare a treasure, then, as Merlin placed it into his hands, he exclaimed 'What is this?'

'It is a sword of great power,' replied Merlin, 'it is called Excalibur.'

Reverently the King drew the sword from its scabbard, and marvelled at how straight and true the blade was, how clean and sharp.

'There is no other sword like it in the world,' said Merlin, 'it is made of a very hard metal, called steel. The runes you can see engraved on the blade are said to give it such power that it is unbreakable and able to strike through steel and stone without blunting. Indeed, the name Excalibur means "cut-steel", while some call it Caliburn or "flashing sword" as it is said to shine like a flaming torch in battle. Feel how its grip fits your hand.'

'It is superbly balanced,' said Arthur, brandishing it with all his strength and making the blade sing in the air, 'this sword, "Excalibur", I shall make my symbol of authority; it will be with me always. My thanks once again, Merlin my true friend; you never fail to amaze me!'

Another and very frequent visitor to Stonehenge was Efflan the High Priest. He had been very eager to see the result of all the hard and lengthy work that had been carried out, and truly believed that Stonehenge had been inspired by the Gods. His sense of relief when all the power and authority of the Blue Stones had been safely embedded within the heart of the great building was immense. The sacred place, where the Solstices meet, was now blessed and hallowed more than ever, and Efflan often came to pray and meditate, gaining great spiritual comfort from the aura that emanated from the stones.

In addition to being a place of worship, he was determined that it should be a centre where truth and justice would flourish, a setting for ceremonial occasions, at which the greatest and wisest folk in the land would have their set places. At this time, Efflan was engaged in drawing up a list of suitable candidates to be allocated permanent seats, including Elders, members of the High Council, tribal Chieftains and others, who he thought possessed the right qualities.

On Efflan's list, however, was the name of none other than Prince Modred. The latter's intrigues and underhand machinations had enabled him to gain himself a reputation as a great organiser and politician, with a deep understanding of state affairs, although Efflan had no real idea of the control he now wielded within the High Council.

Because of his position as a member of the Royal family, Modred had managed to convince many of the Elders that he had significant political influence, and had craftily managed to use this respect from others to achieve his own ends on an increasing number of occasions. As a result, there was now a power within the High Council that was not healthy.

Modred's unseen, but baleful, influence had reached a point where he could dictate, or orchestrate, events as he chose, with no one being aware of the true state of affairs. Even his uncle, the King, preoccupied as he was with other matters, did not perceive the threat that Modred posed. Like so many others, he only considered his nephew to be a harmless, competent and faceless politician. This was to prove a fatal error of judgement.

Chapter Twenty

Modred's whirlwind visit to Stonehenge had set the evil thoughts in his diseased mind swirling and bubbling, in an insane frenzy of desire and lust for total power. Its impact on him had brought matters to a head; he was no longer prepared to wait for his long-term goal of absolute domination, using his customary sly, underhand scheming and manipulation. Alone once more, in his darkened room – apart from the bloated figure of his wart-encrusted pet toad – he gazed up at the image of Cernunnos, which appeared to leer evilly through the clouds of smoke.

'O, Great One, he rasped, 'the time has come for me to act. In the dark hours of the night, you have promised that I shall gain absolute power in this land and all will bow before me. In return, I shall give you a blood sacrifice – my beloved uncle, King Arthur, the only person who stands between me and my ultimate goal!'

At that, Modred began to laugh, as he did at Stonehenge; a high-pitched, hysterical laugh which went on and on, echoing around the room and chilling even the cold blood of his toad, which shuddered and shrank fearfully away into a corner.

Having made his promise, Modred began to review the devious plans, already festering in his black heart.

'My scheme to send my dear, naïve uncle to where Cernunnos awaits him, in the Otherworld, must be completely foolproof,' he thought to himself, 'I cannot trust anyone but myself to strike him down, although I have to appear innocent of the deed. This must be the perfect murder, and I must be the undetectable killer.'

His psychopathic mind raced ahead, as he muttered, 'What I need is a dupe, some fool who will take the blame; but he must not live to tell the truth about what really happened!' Twisting one corner of his mouth up, into something between a smile and a snarl, he added, 'Another gift for Cernunnos – and there will be plenty more before I have done!'

As he paced up and down, deep in thought, he was planning something that involved more than one death. 'Curses!' he spat suddenly, 'I had forgotten that stupid dolt Crelin, who always sleeps outside the Royal bedchamber. He must be removed and got out of the way somehow, but, if he can remain unaware of what is going on, it will not be necessary to kill him. A fool who knows nothing, and will confuse the situation nicely, is of more use to me alive than dead! However, that means I will need a decoy as well as an assumed assassin; let me see, it is said that Crelin has an eye for the ladies... hmm, I wonder...' Lost in concentration, he continued his pacing and plotting.

After a while, Modred suddenly stopped, raised both arms above his head and cried out: 'Glory to Cernunnos! Master, you have inspired me once again; you are so strong within me, that it is as if I, Modred the Magnificent, am actually becoming Cernunnos! Oh, great Horned God, manifest your power in me as I speak!'

He now had the perfect answers, and his plan seemed to him, both complete and foolproof. To deceive Crelin would be easy. One of the few girls who was stupid enough to stay in his service was also very pretty, and so, capable of luring any man from his post.

'I will tell her to make sheep's-eyes at him,' he thought, 'then get him to chase her, so they go well away from the Royal bedchamber. If she surprises him, half asleep, he will run after her without thinking. As for a dupe to take the blame for the assassination, who better than Muir, one of Bullpin's faithful lieutenants? He is big, muscular and powerful, yet as dumb as an ox. His one sign of intelligence is that he worships me, so he will do whatever he is told. He will have his moment in history, yet he won't even know it, before I send him down to where Cernunnos awaits him!'

As he began to realise the full extent of his evil scheme, Modred started to laugh again. Peal after hideous peal rang through his room, as the toad crouched down in fear once more.

'Oh, my dear Uncle,' he gasped eventually, 'if only you knew the treat I have in store for you!'

Once he had chosen his two dupes, Modred rehearsed them in the parts they had to play, without them even dimly suspecting either the appalling outcome of their actions or the fate that awaited them. So terrified of him were they, that they just did as he instructed them, again and again, until they could go through the motions automatically.

The next step was to smuggle them into the Royal Palace without being challenged, in case they blurted out something that might make the guards suspicious.

'I can come and go through the Palace gates as I please,' he thought, 'so these two fools must accompany me. They will be my bodyguards!'

The irony of this caused him much additional amusement, as they eventually made their way to the Palace.

As Modred had anticipated, no one challenged his companions as they passed through the main gates. Indeed, once they saw him approaching, the guards themselves retreated hastily and cleared the way for Prince Modred and his attendants, hoping he would pass by without giving them an evil scowl. Similarly unchallenged, he made his way through a warren of corridors and passages, until all three were standing in the shadows, within sight of the door to the Royal Bedchamber.

As Modred had anticipated, the sleeping figure of King Arthur's servant, Crelin, lay across the doorway, protecting the royal couple. Motioning the girl to fill a cup with water from a nearby basin, Modred then pushed her towards the sleeping figure. For a moment she hesitated, fearful at finding herself alone, but an angry gesture from her master sent the girl scurrying across to stand over Crelin. Now, her own simple sense of humour took over; she saw the sleeping man, snoring with his mouth wide open, as a real figure of fun. What a great joke, she thought, to wake him with a soaking; it would be as funny as the games they played at the fair! So, with one sweep of her arm, she drenched the sleeping Crelin.

He was awake and on his feet in an instant, choking and spluttering in alarm, at what seemed to be a sudden attack from nowhere. Shaking himself and wiping the water from his eyes, Crelin saw nothing but a young girl laughing at him.

'Why, you – you cheeky beggar!' he roared, 'I'll teach you a lesson you won't forget!'

Giggling, the girl wriggled her body at him, then turned and began to run off down the corridor. Still half-blinded and soaking wet, Crelin set off in hot pursuit, with a big grin on his face, determined to make the girl pay for her impudence.

No sooner were they out of sight, around a corner, than Modred promptly opened the door of the Royal Bedchamber and slipped quickly inside. Thinking it was Crelin, King Arthur threw off the fur coverlet and sat up in bed to see what he wanted.

When he saw Modred standing there, however, he let out an oath and was on his feet in an instant, snatching up Excalibur as he rose. Awakened by the sound of his voice, Queen Constance anxiously followed him.

'Modred, explain yourself!' cried the King, 'What is the meaning of your presence, and where is Crelin?'

Modred was all humility and contrition. 'Your Majesty,' he whispered, 'I bring dreadful news. I have discovered that there is a plot to kill you. There are would-be assassins at hand; please conceal yourself at once, and I will protect you.'

Terrified, Queen Constance seized her husband's arm. 'My Lord,' she cried, 'Arthur, my dearest husband, do as he says! Don't let them kill you!'

Calmly but firmly, King Arthur said in a strong voice, 'Modred, protect the Queen. Take her to a place of safety and see that she is well guarded; that is a direct order from your King; do as I command immediately!'

Modred bowed and quickly left the room with Queen Constance, who was now distracted and sobbing bitterly. Hurrying along the corridor with the frantic Queen, Modred reached Princess Guinevere's bedchamber; opening the door, he pushed the Queen inside saying he would call the guards. Then, using a large plank of wood that fitted across the door, he locked them both inside.

Racing back, he halted outside the Royal Bedchamber. For a moment he listened. All was quiet, and he gave a satisfied, wolfish grin, realising that his servant girl had successfully performed the second part of her task, which had been to lure Crelin into an empty room.

'Now,' he thought, 'I am ready to begin the next stage of my brilliant plan.'

In a high, piercing, terrified voice, he began to shout loudly: 'Help! Help! Guards! Come quickly! Sound the alarm; the King's life is in danger!'

Within seconds all was confusion; people were shouting and the guards could be heard running to the outer walls. This suited Modred's schemes perfectly. He turned and grabbed the stupid Muir from his hiding place in the shadows, hissing urgently: 'Follow me; in here, quick!' With a single lunge, he pushed the big man through the doorway of the Royal Bedchamber, where, seeing an unknown intruder bursting in, King Arthur immediately ran him through with Excalibur, killing him instantly.

Modred then swiftly re-entered the room, gasping: 'Thank the Gods, Sire! You are still alive!' For a fatal moment, the King relaxed his guard, laying Excalibur aside. Modred moved closer; in an instant he seized a sharp dagger, hidden under his cloak, and struck like a snake, stabbing the King through the heart. All too late, he realised the awful truth, King Arthur looked into his nephew's eyes, which now glittered with venomous hatred, and read his doom.

'You stupid fool,' hissed Modred, 'die; it is my destiny to take your place!' He struck again and again, frenziedly gasping 'Die, I say! Die! Cernunnos awaits you!'

When he looked down, King Arthur's bloodstained body lay lifeless at his feet.

In the very moment of his triumph, Modred knew that, even now, there was not a second to lose. He took the dagger and ran down the corridor to where the servant girl was waiting, outside the door against which Crelin was vainly beating.

Grabbing her, he cried loudly, 'Look out, she has a knife; stop her, she is mad!' By now the Palace was in an uproar and, in the universal pandemonium, with everyone's attention distracted, he forced the girl to face the wall, and with a single swift motion of the dagger, cut her throat. Her body fell to the ground as though she had fainted, and he threw a cloak over her to hide the blood, until he was far away from the scene.

Confusion reigned everywhere that night, until eventually, the Senior Elder, Durrel, managed to take control. 'Guards,' he shouted, 'get everyone into the Banqueting Hall immediately, and make sure no one gets out until I give the order! Meanwhile, I will go and find the King!'

Durrel then rushed to the Royal Bedchamber, where, to his utter horror, he found King Arthur and another unknown man, lying dead, in pools of their own blood. To add to Durrel's bewilderment, the King's faithful servant, Crelin, was nowhere to be found, and while searching the corridors, he had stumbled across a third corpse; that of a servant girl, lying in a huddled heap a short distance away.

'The unbelievable has happened; King Arthur is dead!' he thought despairingly; 'How has this ghastly triple tragedy occurred? Who is responsible?'

Further searches resulted in the release of Queen Constance and Princess Guinevere, as well as Crelin from the chamber where the girl had entrapped him; he had been locked in and, by now, he was frantic with worry. It was Durrel's grievous task to inform them of King Arthur's death, and he did so with the heaviest of hearts.

On hearing the news, the queen fainted. She and the Princess were inconsolable, in disbelief that something so horrible could have happened. Crelin could not forgive himself; the one time in all his years of service that he had left his customary post, his Royal Master had been foully murdered. Why had he deserted his own faithful Master? Despite all attempts to reassure him, Crelin felt that he had betrayed his King and wandered off, alone, in the depths of despair.

When the first shock had passed, Durrel realised that it was his responsibility to begin an official inquiry into the deaths straight away. Knowing that this might take some time, and that people could not be kept confined in the Banqueting Hall indefinitely, he gave further orders that no one must leave the Palace until the truth had been discovered.

Once the bodies had been removed and treated with due reverence, Durrel began to question the weeping Queen Constance, along with Modred, whose very presence in the Palace on this occasion, raised suspicions in his mind. Princess Guinevere, he had decided, was too young and too distraught to be interrogated; besides, she had obviously seen nothing of the murders.

The Queen tearfully managed to tell Durrel how Modred had helped her escape her husband's fate. Next, Durrel turned to Modred and asked 'How, your Highness, did you know there was a plot to kill the King?'

'I saw the girl distract Crelin and lure him away from the door of His Majesty's room,' he replied, with every appearance of shocked and grief-stricken innocence, 'and then a furtive-looking man appeared carrying a dagger. He was about to enter the Royal bedchamber when I confronted him. He immediately called for assistance, so I assumed that he was not alone. It was then that I rushed in, to warn the King and Queen of the danger.'

Durrel thought for a few moments, then asked pensively, 'Who killed the girl?' To this, Modred gave his well-rehearsed reply, saying simply: 'I don't know; she was obviously part of the whole vile plot. I had to protect the Queen, but, when I went back to see the King again, the villain had stabbed him to death. In his attempt to escape, he attacked me, also, so I had to kill him in self-defence; it was him or me; I had no choice!'

There was a short pause before Durrel spoke again. 'That is all very well,' he said, 'but it still does not answer my question as to who killed the girl.'

'It must have been the assassin,' replied Modred quickly, 'he would have had to do it to cover his tracks, so that she could not give him away.'

At this point Queen Constance intervened, saying 'Modred, I owe you my life. Thank you for saving me.'

Modred tried to look suitably noble, and replied: 'Your Majesty, I will endeavour to continue to protect you and your lovely daughter, the Princess, and to ensure that no one will hurt either of you, whilst I am alive.'

With Durrel's official enquiry finally at an end, he told everyone in the Palace to go about their normal duties, even though he knew it would not be easy. Arrangements were made for King Arthur's body to lie in state and for a period of mourning to be observed.

Since the country now lacked a ruler, Modred seized the opportunity to take control. As he was now the only surviving male member of the Royal family, no one dared to question his authority. His first step was to arrange a meeting of the High Council, to inform everyone officially of the tragic blow that had been struck at the safety, stability and welfare of the Kingdom. Modred then followed this by ordering that the Queen and Princess Guinevere should be locked away from any contact with the outside world, feigning that this step was to be taken for their own safety.

Chapter Twenty-one

While the remainder of the Kingdom was still in grief, Modred was in good humour.

'Now,' he gleefully thought to himself, 'I am in sole control of the realm! My word, alone, is law, and I have the power of life or death over the entire population! My Lord Cernunnos rules through me; I feel his power running through every vein in my body! But I must proceed with caution; there are many who mourn King Arthur and have no love for me – some with good reason!'

He smiled evilly, thinking of those, who, having displeased him, were now languishing in his dungeons, providing sport for Potter, Bullpin and their minions.

'Yes,' he murmured, 'the Age of Modred is dawning, but I must proceed with care. The High Council are effectively in my power now, and I can use them as a smokescreen, so the people believe that they and I rule the country together, while in reality, all decisions will be mine and mine alone!'

However, there was still one obstacle Modred had to consider in his attempt to grasp absolute power, and that was the figure of Merlin. Concentrating entirely on his experiments, deep in the forest, Merlin had been totally unaware of the tragic events at the Royal Palace.

His absence at such a time was marked by many, and Modred, at one point, considered somehow throwing the blame for the tragedy on him, but even his twisted, psychopathic mind told him that this would be going too far.

'I will find a way to deal with him later,' thought Modred, 'he of all people will have no place in my glorious new order.'

Then, as part of his smokescreen hiding his true intentions from the people, he considered it important to be seen keeping on good terms with the priestly establishment and particularly with the High Priest, Efflan.

'I will be accepted more readily by my subjects as a man of faith,' he reasoned to himself, 'and Efflan is a gullible old fool, who I can easily hoodwink. If he only knew at whose shrine I really worship!'

Shortly afterwards, he issued an invitation, in his own hand, to Efflan; requesting him to attend a private meeting, which he knew would flatter the old High Priest.

When they were alone together, Modred began in low, grieving tones, 'Your Reverence, what a tragic situation we find ourselves in! This is when the whole country will need

221

you. Will you arrange for the King to lie in state and then be given a suitably Royal funeral?'

The old man nodded sadly.

'Also, Efflan,' Modred went on, 'will you help me to hold the country together at this time of great need? I shall rely on you, greatly, in the sad times ahead.'

'Yes, certainly, Prince,' replied Efflan, 'I will make all the funeral arrangements and do all in my power to help you in the future.'

They parted on the best of terms; Modred was certain that he now had an ally whose support would help establish his rule.

Meanwhile, Merlin had finally heard the terrible tidings of King Arthur's murder. He was devastated by the death of his closest friend, and fearful that there would be very little time before Modred seized total control. However strong his own personal feelings of grief and loss, he knew he had to set these aside and act straight away, to try and remedy matters. The situation was desperate, and required equally desperate measures to deal with it.

Convinced that Modred was involved in the King's death, most probably the one responsible for it, he went at once to see Durrel, whom he knew to be an honest man and completely trustworthy. When they were alone together and could not be overheard, Merlin explained that it was absolutely necessary for him to examine the bodies of King Arthur, the man and the girl.

'I know this may seem wrong and disrespectful to the dead,' Merlin went on, 'but I also know the King would have demanded that we take whatever steps are necessary to discover the truth of this dreadful affair, regardless of how painful or difficult it may be.'

Convinced by Merlin's words, Durrel wasted no time. A secure room was set aside for Merlin's use, and the three bodies were secretly conveyed there. The King was laid on a table, covered from head to foot; the bodies of the man and the girl, similarly covered, were positioned on another table nearby. All three bodies had been placed where they could be clearly seen by means of daylight coming from directly overhead.

'Please leave me now,' said Merlin to Durrel, who had enquired if there was anything further he needed, 'I must do what I have to do.' Tears were in his eyes as he spoke. Durrel left the room quietly and fastened the door securely behind him.

Merlin took a deep breath and steeled himself for what lay ahead. First of all, he removed the coverings from the man and the girl. The girl had a gaping wound across her throat, which Merlin could tell had been made with a single slash from behind with a sharp, narrow blade. The

223

man had been run through with a single sword thrust that had penetrated his heart. From the size of the wound, Merlin knew that this was the work of Excalibur. King Arthur had defended himself to some purpose, yet he, too, now lay dead.

Since he was the only living being in this room of death, Merlin could weep openly as he started to examine his friend, saying to him 'I am so sorry this dreadful thing has happened. Please forgive me; I have to look at your fatal wounds.' Merlin carefully cut away the King's clothing and examined the numerous small puncture holes in his chest. On the table beside him, he had laid a dagger that belonged to the other man, Muir. Already, he had noticed that there was no blood on the blade of the weapon, or any traces of it on Muir's hands. In fact, the only blood on this man was that which had obviously flowed from his own fatal wound. If he had used his dagger to commit murder, his arm would be soaked in the King's blood.

Merlin then had to attempt to insert the weapon into his friend's heart. He had to summon up all his resolve to undertake this gruesome task, but on making a start, he found that the puncture holes were too small to have been made by the dagger he held in his hand.

'There!' muttered Merlin, 'we now have proof that Muir was not the murderer. It is obvious that King Arthur killed Muir with Excalibur, but someone else killed the King. It certainly was not the girl!'

He was convinced he knew the identity of the real murderer, but proving it would be a different matter.

Merlin, therefore, still had much to consider and despite the traumatic but essential physical examination being completed, it was with a heavy heart that he said farewell to his most dear friend and reverently replaced the covers over the three bodies. Outside, Durrel was still keeping watch, to prevent any intrusion until Merlin had completed his tragic task.

'It is finished,' Merlin told him, 'I have done what I had to do. My thanks, Durrel, you have served your King well! I beg you, tell no one of what has passed here today. Now I must leave the Palace, but I shall send word to you, again, before long.'

Meanwhile, Modred continued plotting his evil schemes. King Arthur's death was not, in itself, enough for him; Queen Constance remained, and could become a rallying-point for opposition to his rule.

'Another sacrifice beckons,' he thought, 'but this time there must be no wounds, no blood. Poison is the answer in her case!' Murderer that he was, Modred had experimented for years with poisons he had personally concocted and administered. 'Something fairly slow – not too slow, but

225

eventually fatal, I think,' he mused, 'and with no bitter taste that might make her suspicious. I will tell the Elders that she is pining with grief, and show her in public from time to time so that no one suspects foul play. If they question anything, I will tell them she is dying of a broken heart – how romantic!'

Having made up his mind, Modred did not hesitate. In her virtual captivity, Queen Constance was still filled with grief; she ate and drank very little, and cared even less about it. Modred ordered one of the women guarding her – she and the Princess were surrounded only by his creatures now – to persuade her into taking daily doses of what he said was a special cordial to keep her strength up.

The Queen was inevitably suspicious at first, but the drink tasted pleasant and seemed to have no apparent side-effects, so she started to take it regularly. After a short while, however, she began to look paler and paler as the days passed, and by the time the Royal funeral took place, she could hardly stand. Princess Guinevere felt lost without her father; she missed him terribly, but all she was able to do was to console and nurse her mother as best she could, and grieve still more as Queen Constance wasted away.

She did not even consider that Modred might have plans for her as well, or what those evil plans might be. She was unaware of how completely in his power she was, and that her situation could not be worse.

Chapter Twenty-two

The closing stages of that tragic year brought some of the worst weather anyone could remember. King Arthur's death was followed by grey, leaden skies and torrential rain which lashed down constantly, driven by cold, gale force winds.

'Life can be very cruel,' thought Merlin sadly. He knew full well the peril the country was in, but was powerless to change things; all he could do was wait and allow events to unfold. His best friend, the most honoured man in the country, was dead; lying in state, King Arthur awaited a funeral ceremony that was due to take place on the day of the Winter Solstice. Queen Constance's health was declining daily; there was even doubt, now, as to whether she would be able to attend the burial. Meanwhile, she and Princess Guinevere were virtual prisoners, kept in close confinement by Modred 'for their own safety', as he put it.

Even now though, Modred hesitated to move openly and reveal the full extent of his desire for absolute power. While his subjects filed past the King's body, Arthur's authority could still be felt, and Modred feared a national uprising if he struck too soon.

'Patience, patience,' he thought, 'thanks to my Lord Cernunnos, I have come this far. He has filled my body with his power, so I can become more like him. I can afford to wait until my poor dear late uncle's corpse is safely in the ground and his Queen has joined him before I reveal myself. Only then will the people see my true magnificence!' Successfully concealing his impatience and contempt for everyone else, Modred made sure that he was seen to be ostentatiously grieving, as often as possible, in the period before the royal funeral.

By the time the day of the Winter Solstice dawned, the rain had turned to snow and several heavy falls had transformed the landscape into an eerie white world where the only sounds were the howling of the wind and the menacing calls of ravens flying overhead.

Then, suddenly, came the sad, subdued throb of muffled drums, heralding the appearance of King Arthur's funeral cortege, moving slowly out through the Palace gates. The body, covered in long, sombre funeral drapery embroidered with scenes of mourning, was carried, shoulder high on a bier, by members of the High Council and Senior Chieftains, who took this sad duty in turns. The King's gold, jewel-studded crown and his wondrous sword Excalibur had also been laced on the bier as symbols of his power and authority.

Close behind, carried in a litter because of her frailty, came Queen Constance and Princess Guinevere, with Modred in close attendance. Accompanying the Royal family were a small number of Elders, senior Ministers and members of the Royal Household. There were less than a hundred people in the procession, all told, as the unexpected suddenness of the King's death had left insufficient time for foreign dignitaries to attend. All present were heavily muffled up against the cold, and many were swathed in furs, while the thick snow lying under foot made progress slow.

Despite the bitter cold, many ordinary folk, including Whittle and his family, had ventured out to stand, with bare heads, in the falling snow and pay their respects to the King, as he passed by for the last time. As the procession slowly wound its way to the sacred royal burial place, the contrast between the pure white snow and the sombre darkness of the little band of moving figures had a sad, haunting beauty, which reduced many of the spectators to tears. There was a universal feeling of loss, and that something good had gone out of their lives for ever.

At the royal burial enclosure, Efflan and his priests were waiting, their white robes blending with the blanket of snow. It was a pure and peaceful place, with the large barrows and upright memorial stones providing some shelter from the bitter wind. When the funeral procession arrived at the freshly prepared burial chamber it halted, and King Arthur's body was carefully lifted from the bier and placed on a wooden trestle.

Then the ceremony began, according to time-honoured custom, with Efflan as High Priest, reciting the sacred rites for the dead and making a speech, in which he praised King Arthur's merits and mourned his untimely loss. Out of consideration for the sick Queen and others, obviously suffering in the severe weather, he kept this brief, as did Modred and, after him, Durrel, as Senior Elder, when subsequently called upon to speak. Merlin, who was also among the mourners, had arranged to remain silent, in the background, and to let Arthur be laid to rest among his own people.

When the time came for the King's body to be placed in the burial chamber, it was lifted from the trestle and arranged in its ordained position by the priests, with great reverence. To provide for his comfort in the Otherworld, various items of grave goods were then carefully distributed around him, while the priests sang a lament. His favourite gold ring was placed on his finger, while beside him was put his personal dagger together with axe-heads from his early life. Also accompanying him were his hunting bow, arrows and spear. There were many items made of gold including a large, flat, crescent-shaped votive necklace, of very finely beaten gold, called a lunula, and a beautiful golden torc, for his arrival in the Otherworld. The final item was King Arthur's own drinking cup, cut from a single block of amber, which glowed in the light reflected from the snow, as though it was illuminated from within.

Meanwhile, Modred, while maintaining his air of pious grief, was watching the grave goods being placed in the burial chamber and thinking 'What a waste! Those gold objects would grace my magnificence to far greater effect! I do not care! I will have lots more to comfort me, including his greatest treasure – the Princess Guinevere – along with his other belongings. Maybe, when people have forgotten about the old fool, I can get Potter or Bullpin to dig them up for me! Now let's get a move on and finish this jabbering nonsense; I'm cold, and I need a drink - to celebrate his departure!'

Some distance away was the miserable figure of Crelin, crouching down and half-hidden by a large stone monument. He had followed his Master to the last, and now felt he had come to the end of his own journey through life.

'There is no future for me,' he thought, 'it is my fault the King is dead; he has gone, and I serve no purpose in remaining behind. Maybe in the Otherworld I can find forgiveness!'

He sank down in the snow and wept bitterly, then turned, unseen by the others, and crept away, to where a tall, bare tree stood alone, silhouetted against the sky, high above on the escarpment. Halting here, he pulled a length of stout rope from under his cloak. Tying one end to a strong branch, he quickly fashioned a running noose from the other. Then, placing the noose about his neck and pulling it tight, he closed his eyes and jumped over the edge.

Many hours later, his absence was noticed and a search party was organised. Spotting a single line of footprints in the snow, leading away from the burial site, the searchers followed these until they came in sight of the lone tree, which, they saw to their horror, now bore a hanging figure that dangled and swung in the wind. Crelin had finally joined his Master in the Otherworld!

Meanwhile, the Winter Solstice sun was setting on the horizon, turning the snow an ominous blood-red, and the funeral ceremony had come to an end. Massive slabs of stone were laid across the top of the burial chamber, ready for the raising of the mound of earth that would make the Royal barrow complete. Attendants carried the litter containing the distraught Queen and Princess, whose heartbroken sobbing could be clearly heard from within, back to the Palace, and other members of the funeral party slipped quietly away, a few at a time, wishing to be alone with their memories.

Only Merlin remained, a single, dark sentinel, standing motionless, in the heavily falling snow, beside the grave. 'Arthur, I must go now,' he said softly, 'even though you are in the spirit world, I shall carry you with me always – but more than that, you will become immortal, and the legend of King Arthur shall live for ever!'

He bowed low, then turned and walked slowly away, into the gathering gloom.

Chapter Twenty-three

Following the terrible murder of King Arthur, the entire nation was gripped by a sense of fear and uncertainty. Soon after his funeral, Queen Constance finally succumbed to Modred's insidious poison and died, and was later buried beside her husband. Her distraught daughter, Princess Guinevere, was kept in close confinement, locked away from public view.

People shuddered at the thought, but it appeared there was a strong possibility that Modred would become King, by default, or otherwise the country would be at the mercy of any foreign would-be conqueror. As a result of his years of scheming and manipulation, Modred was now master of what he had always sought – absolute power.

He had amassed an army, mainly composed of thieves, bullies and outlaws, while his personal bodyguard, under the infamous duo of Potter and Bullpin, were little more than a band of cut-throats, hired killers and fellow-murderers. There were insufficient loyal forces to mount any form of opposition, or to have any hope of overthrowing him. Little by little he had taken over the country, until he stood alone at its head, a figure of evil, whom no one appeared able to withstand. Modred had even committed the ultimate blasphemy and taken over Stonehenge, turning it into a gigantic shrine to Cernunnos, his Lord of Darkness.

All those in high office had failed to realise what Modred was planning, and had turned a blind eye for too long, but, now, it had become terrifyingly obvious. Efflan was as culpable as the others; the old High Priest realised with grief and remorse what was happening, but it was too late. Now, in fear of his life from Modred's psychotic rages, he, like the others, just had to do what he was told.

As with the priesthood, the High Council were also firmly in Modred's clutches, while the Chieftains were so scattered about the country, and so disorganised, that they found themselves unable to mount any form of united resistance. Along with the Elders, they could only wait and watch for an opportunity to arise when they could make a stand against him. But, without any obvious leader, they were powerless to do anything.

Meanwhile, Merlin was working in secret, making plans and building his resources to mount an effective challenge against Modred's evil rule. During King Arthur's funeral, he had found an opportunity to secrete both the Royal crown and the sword Excalibur, key symbols of Royal power and authority, and to carry them away to a safe hiding-place. So expertly had he done this, that no one had been aware of it at the time, and so, after the funeral, both crown and sword could not be found! On hearing this, Modred had flown into a towering rage and vented his fury in a threat to kill everyone, but all to no avail; his peremptory demand that they be found and brought to him, instantly, produced no result whatsoever.

Despite Merlin's secrecy, Modred suspected that he was behind this setback in some way and kept him closely confined, although, even he, did not dare to attempt to have him killed. Merlin's every movement was being spied upon, however, and those who dared to visit him in his prison-like quarters did so at their peril.

Boy, who had been horror-struck by the King's assassination, was determined to talk with Merlin even if it meant risking his life in the attempt. Anything was better than watching lawlessness and evil spreading over the land without being able to lift a finger to prevent it. He managed to smuggle himself into the Palace, undetected, and enter Merlin's room, where he was overjoyed to see his mentor again.

The feeling was mutual. 'I am glad you came,' said Merlin, with a glint of hope in his eye, 'I need your help, Boy.'

They talked in low voices for over an hour, undisturbed, while the watching eyes of Modred's security guards thought that he was alone. Merlin explained that as things stood, all he could do at present was to use his position to gather and analyse all useful information. Boy, however, with all the courage and impatience of youth, wanted to act immediately.

'No,' said Merlin, shaking his head, 'that is not possible at present; it would be too dangerous as things stand. What I would suggest you do is arrange a meeting with your father Whittle and tell him to gather round him as many loyal Chieftains as he can. I will do the same with all my friends and supporters. As soon as we are ready, I will somehow arrange to give my guards the slip and we can all meet together when the moon is full.'

Boy asked only one question, 'Where?'

Merlin replied: 'The gateway'.

Following their meeting, from which Boy was fortunately able to escape unseen, as easily as he had arrived, both had much to organise. Boy found that his father was only too ready to help in the fight against Modred, and the response from the trusted Chieftains, with whom he spoke, was overwhelming. Merlin, too, met with determined support from those he approached.

The night of the full moon finally arrived, and at the appointed time, all the people in authority gathered together, shielded from prying eyes, deep in the hollow of the gateway. All the people from Whittle's tribe were on guard, hidden in every tree and bush within sight, as protection for the meeting place. Those attending included Brenon, the High Chieftain, and Durrel, the Senior Elder, along with other members of the High Council – all those who had seen through Modred's lies. Chieftains and leaders were all of one mind: to agree somehow to bring down Modred.

When all were present, Merlin was the first to greet them, saying, 'I am glad to see you all; this is a brave act, as we risk our lives being here. You know the evils of Modred's rule; although he has not yet declared himself officially to be our ruler, he is responsible for the appalling state of the country. Things could not be worse at the present time; Modred is not only insane, but he is also a killer. I have carried out a medical examination on the bodies of the man and woman involved. I also examined the body of my dear beloved friend, King Arthur. My investigations show that the King killed the so-called assassin, Muir, so, obviously, he could not have commited the murder, which conclusively proves that the real killer of King Arthur was someone else – I believe that person to be none other than Modred himself!' A low, growling, roar of anger ran round the assembled throng, then they quickly fell silent once more.

Merlin continued, 'We have no choice; we cannot reason with him, therefore we must fight – and fight to kill!'

There came a call from the shadows: 'Let's attack now; I would rather die, than live knowing that the evil swine killed our King!'

A ripple of agreement followed, but Merlin quickly asked for calm, saying, 'I know you are all angry – and you shall have your revenge, but, to be successful, it will take time and the essential thing is that we must all work together. Modred has strong defences and many highly organised and ruthless men at his command. It will take meticulous planning and organisation to defeat him. The main thing we shall have to our advantage is the element of surprise. Our plans must therefore remain secret, at all costs, so that at the critical moment, when we strike, we will catch him completely off guard!'

After considerable discussion, they had to admit that Merlin's approach carried the greatest chance of success. Then, they gradually dispersed in small groups, slipping silently away through the shadows, to avoid being caught in the bright moonlight.

Meanwhile, Modred was revelling in his new-found status. Not yet daring to seize the throne outright, he had arranged to have himself appointed Head of the High

Council. Now, over his customary black attire, he wore magnificent robes, made of cloth of gold and richly embroidered, and strutted around, festooned with gold chains and badges studded with precious stones.

He was talking and acting more wildly and uncontrollably than ever before, but, the late King's Ministers were powerless to do anything to curb his excesses without a monarch to authorise their actions. Modred was fully aware of their views, but cared nothing for them. These people were all less than the dust, mere slaves to do his bidding. But, even with his sick mind, he could also see the other side's point of view: that to seize power, without first finding himself some form of legitimacy, would, in all probability, give him problems he did not care to consider.

'Being the King's nephew is not enough,' he thought. 'As the Chosen One of Cernunnos, I can obviously award myself any title I like, but, I must be seen to have a valid claim to the throne. Those stupid foreign rulers are bound to stick their noses into my affairs; they will need to be reassured, of course; I don't want to have to fight them while I'm still making ready for outright war! I will crush them after they have come to witness and fear my magnificence!'

Brooding alone, in his dark, forbidding chamber, he twisted the subject around in his slippery mind. 'Legitimacy, legitimacy,' he muttered. Then he thought of his captive, the Princess Guinevere, and was so pleased that he began shrieking and croaking with laughter, like some bird of ill-omen.

'When we are married,' he cried out, 'I will become King Modred! The ceremony will make me a true Royal Sovereign, and my title will be secure for as long as I need it!' He hugged himself with his bony arms and rocked to and fro in glee. 'No one will ever be able to question anything I do ever again. I can just see the looks on their stupid faces!'

Then another thought struck him. 'I will have children by her and found a new dynasty, which will rule this benighted, backward country for ever. Won't she be overjoyed, when I tell her what the future holds for her! She will make a very beautiful Queen and I shall enjoy founding my dynasty!' He smiled a crooked, leering smile, then, being in good humour, he rose to fetch some particularly revolting-looking insect, as a treat for his pet Toad, who devoured it greedily.

'So shall I devour my opponents!' he gloated.

Modred's next step was to inform Efflan of his plans for the ceremony, which would combine his wedding to Princess Guinevere with his coronation as King.

'Naturally,' he said grandly, it will be held at Stonehenge; that is the perfect place for such a State occasion.'

The old High Priest went very pale and shuddered at the thought of how King Arthur's and Merlin's superb building would become so foully desecrated, but realised, sadly, that he had no choice in the matter.

'Before that, of course,' Modred's rasping voice broke into his thoughts, 'the people must be made accustomed to the idea. I propose to have the Princess put on public display, so that all can see her. This will make her even more popular than she was before, and the spectators will realise how suitable she is to be my bride!' He began to give detailed instructions to Efflan as to how this could best be achieved, so that the people would be able to go to Stonehenge and worship her as his consort-to-be.

The original purpose of Stonehenge had now been perverted; it had become a temple to Cernunnos and a very sinister place indeed. A huge image of the Horned God had been placed where it dominated everything else. Large candles burned before it, and an acrid smoke rose from an altar fire, whose flickering flames made it seem as though the image was moving its eyes and assessing the potential victims gathered below.

The apex of the building had been covered over, so that no daylight penetrated the interior. A thick, long pole now descended from the apex to the centre of the Great Hall, with a throne-like seat suspended on it, in mid-air, some distance from the floor. This seat had been designed so that it appeared to be floating, with no visible means of support. Huge candles, sited on each Blue Stone, dimly and eerily illuminated the great open interior, while groups of priests stood in the shadows, chanting verses in praise of Modred's magnificence.

Meanwhile, arrangements had been made for Princess Guinevere to be dressed all in white, drugged and carried to Stonehenge. On arrival, her limp body was forced, by the priests, up a set of stairs and into the high seat. Her wrists and ankles were tied, then she was gagged, to prevent her crying out and, lastly, her face was covered with a veil, so that the gag could not be seen. The staircase was then removed, and the Princess was forced to sit there for hours on end, as a public spectacle, bound hand and foot and in fear of her life.

Later in the day, the main doors were opened and people were allowed inside. They huddled together, in the dim glimmer of the candles, unable to see anything, until a shaft of light, from a previously concealed hole in the roof, suddenly shone down like a spotlight and illuminated the Princess.

Everyone looked up in amazement; the scene had been staged so cunningly that she appeared to be a supernatural apparition, seated amid shining light, like a goddess, with Cernunnos leering down at her through the billowing smoke that rose behind.

Modred, himself, then appeared dramatically out of the darkness and addressed the crowd, crying: 'Rejoice, my people, rejoice! There is to be a Royal Wedding! Princess Guinevere has consented to become my bride. She will be my Queen and I shall be your King, so there will once again be a Royal Family to carry on the line. Rejoice, I say again, rejoice!'

The priests began to applaud and the people, completely stunned by this sudden fearsome revelation, reluctantly began to join in.

Chapter Twenty-four

Finally, Princess Guinevere, half-dead from fear and exhaustion, was released from the indignity of being made a degrading public spectacle and carried back to the Palace. Here, her bonds and gag were removed, and, when sensation began to creep back into her numb limbs and her head had cleared somewhat, she was filled with a burning sense of shame and anger at what had been done to her.

'Never,' she thought, 'never will I even consider marrying that foul brute. The very sight of him makes me feel sick!'

Then, she flung herself down on her hard, narrow bed and wept bitterly, before falling into a mercifully deep sleep.

Her feelings, however, were of no account. Modred's desires and commands were now paramount, and he began to press ahead with organising the wedding preparations as quickly as possible. Guinevere was terrified, yet had no idea what to do. She wanted someone she could trust to confide in, and she desperately needed help, to get away from the terrible fate that awaited her.

Those around her, men and women, were all, without exception, Modred's creatures, who would not allow her to do anything unless she was under close supervision. She felt like a prisoner, and was determined to die rather than marry Modred. If she could find a way, the only plan she could think of, if all else failed, was to commit suicide.

Merlin was horror-stricken when he heard of Modred's evil act, and felt overwhelming compassion for the Princess. 'My first priority,' he thought, 'must be to give the poor child some comfort, by getting word to her that help is on its way. I think I know how to contrive that, but I shall need Efflan's help if I am to succeed.'

The first step was to arrange a secret meeting with the High Priest. Then, when they were face to face and Efflan had expressed his delight at seeing Merlin unharmed, the latter explained his plan, saying: 'We have to make an excuse for you to see the Princess, and arrange for Boy to accompany you. This is essential, because otherwise, she may think that you are part of Modred's vile schemes, but I know she will listen to Boy.'

'A very wise move,' replied Efflan.

'Now,' went on Merlin, 'the next step will be for us to meet with Modred and get his agreement. It will be unpleasant, as always, but these days he is more dangerous than ever. However, I have just the suggestion that I believe will appeal to his warped mind.'

The two men lowered their voices and remained deep in conversation for a while, with Efflan occasionally nodding his head and muttering, 'Excellent, excellent, most ingenious!'

Modred received them with his customary bad-tempered impatience, remembering, with difficulty, that he still had need of Efflan.

'Well, what do you want?' he snapped, furious at seeing the two of them together, and instantly convinced they were plotting something.

Merlin replied soothingly, 'We come here on behalf of the Princess Guinevere.'

Modred glared, then rasped angrily, 'Answer my question; what do you want?'

'Do you realise,' said Merlin solemnly, 'the wedding has not been blessed, and it will therefore be unholy?'

This made Modred even angrier. 'What do you mean?' he snarled.

'Her body will have to be prepared and cleansed for matrimony,' explained Merlin.

Despite his rage, this stopped Modred in his tracks. It was something he had not considered, and with which he was forced to agree. Everything had to be done in accordance with religious custom. On reflection, in fact, he found that the idea appealed to him; the thought of Guinevere's body raised lascivious images in his mind.

'Yes, yes!' he blurted out, 'her body prepared – I like that! Efflan, I order you to prepare the Princess – for the Royal coupling.' 'Yes,' he murmured again, lost in thought for a moment, then came back to his senses. 'Now, get out!' Waving his hand, he dismissed them from his presence. 'I have important matters to attend to.'

The following day, Efflan left his chamber at the appointed time, dressed in his ceremonial white robes and sash, holding his Staff of Office and carrying a pot of burning incense. Walking in procession behind him, was another figure, also robed in white, but with his head reverently covered and bearing two large pitchers of sacred water. Under this disguise was none other than Boy; Merlin's plan was working well.

They entered the Palace and went directly to the chamber where the Princess was confined, without being stopped or questioned. When they arrived, they ordered the servants guarding the Princess to leave, to which, their reply was that they had direct orders from Modred to stay with her at all times.

At this, Efflan drew himself up, looked very stern, and using all the authority vested in him as High Priest, insisted on their departure. 'Leave us instantly,' he thundered, 'or be condemned forever! Prince Modred, himself, has agreed that the Princess must be cleansed!' Faced with this ultimatum, and the use of Modred's name, they quickly scurried out of the room.

The unfortunate Princess looked thin, pale and wan, and was dressed only in a flimsy night robe. Her first reaction on seeing the two visitors was one of fear; she had learned to mistrust everyone.

Efflan spoke softly, to try and reassure her, saying: 'Princess Guinevere, do not be afraid, we are here to help you.' However, she appeared to be in a lost, trance-like state, seemingly incapable of understanding what he was saying. She just looked dully at Efflan, without replying, standing in silence, as though to afraid to talk.

All this time, Boy had been standing with his covered head bowed down and his eyes fixed on the floor. Then, surprised by the silence, he looked up. He was stunned!

'This cannot be the Princess,' he said to himself, 'there has been a mistake! This is the girl I danced with at the party!' Then he gently whispered, 'Grainne, is it you?' Guinevere turned and looked at him for an instant. Then recognition flashed into her eyes, and she cried out, 'Yes, oh yes, it is me!'

Still completely bewildered, Boy replied, 'Whatever are you doing here?' Catching hold of his arms, she just stammered, 'Boy, please, please help me!' and burst into tears. She sobbed her heart out, with all the grief of losing her parents and all the other misfortunes that had befallen her over the last few months. Boy just held her in his arms.

With great relief, Efflan assured the Princess, 'We are all working to rescue you. Merlin has organised a way to get you out of this horrific situation.' Boy also reassured her, saying: 'Don't worry, we will not let you down; be strong, and know that help is on its way. Meanwhile, just go along with whatever they say. The time for us to strike will be on the wedding day itself!'

Efflan, who had been keeping guard at the door, then turned and said: 'Come quickly, we must leave now.' Boy held his "Grainne" one last time; they looked into each other's eyes and Boy said: 'I love you'.

After sending word to Modred that the ritual cleansing had been satisfactorily completed, Efflan and Boy were able to take advantage of the general confusion, caused by the wedding preparations, to visit Merlin and report back to him.

'All went well,' said Efflan, 'she is safe for the time being, and much relieved to learn of our plan to rescue her on the wedding day.'

Boy then looked at Merlin, and said accusingly, 'You knew all the time that Grainne was the Princess; why did you not tell me?'

'What did it matter?' replied Merlin smiling, 'She is who she is, regardless of her title.' Boy was flabbergasted. Merlin continued, 'Never mind that now, we must make ready for our attack. I will make sure I am inside Stonehenge on the day, as will you, Efflan, together with most of the Elders, High Council and Chieftains. No doubt, we will be searched on entry. That only leaves Whittle and his group of warriors who will be ready to attack and storm the building.'

On the night before the wedding, Merlin and Boy prayed together, silently. Finally, Merlin spoke, saying: 'You will need this.' From its secret hiding-place, he produced the sword Excalibur and handed it to him. 'This was King Arthur's sword,' he said gravely, 'use it, and let the power which lies within it avenge King Arthur's death!'

Boy took the sword, and examined it with awe. Whirling it round his head, he exclaimed: 'It is superbly crafted, so light and well balanced!' Merlin replied with a note of warning, 'Beware of the power you hold in your hands; use it well, my friend.'

They walked, together, into the night; two shadows crossing the open plain. No one saw them as they reached Stonehenge, where they crouched for a moment, to ensure the coast was clear. Merlin put his hand on Boy's shoulder.

'Good luck!' he said, 'we are all depending on you; be not afraid, your destiny awaits you!'

When Boy looked round, Merlin had disappeared. He was on his own now. Following Merlin's instructions, he found two planks of wood, hidden in the undergrowth. Putting these, together with Excalibur, over his shoulder he very carefully and quietly started to climb the huge roof of Stonehenge. So as not to slip, he had first removed his shoes. Slowly, he gradually reached the top and slid the planks under the covers. He next stretched the planks across the opening of the apex, all without making a sound.

Boy then climbed onto the planks and carefully lay down on them, very well aware, that high as he was, in the apex of the building, it was a very long way down to the ground. He knew that all the priests would be fast asleep, in the outer chambers of Stonehenge; thankfully they had not heard a thing.

It was going to be a long, cold and sleepless night, so he wrapped himself up in his cloak. So far, everything had gone according to Merlin's plan; he was ready, and all he had to do now – was wait.

Chapter Twenty-five

On the morning of her wedding, Princess Guinevere was frantic with grief and fear. She had not slept, at all, the previous night, but tossed and turned feverishly, burying her face in the pillow, already wet with her tears, when menaced by nightmarish spectres that loomed at her out of the darkness.

'Oh, Father,' she sobbed, 'what should be the happiest day of my life is going to be one of the most horrible I have ever known! Boy is very brave and means well, but what can one young man and Merlin do, against someone as powerful as Modred?'

She closed her eyes, tight, hoping against hope that the past weeks had been just a bad dream. But no, when she opened her eyes again, she was in the same cramped chamber as before, and the day of her shame and degradation was beginning to dawn.

'This must be how people condemned to death feel, on the morning of their execution,' she thought, as she stood listlessly, with head bowed down, as her captors fitted her into what, on any other occasion, she would have considered a beautiful white gown. Once she was dressed to their satisfaction, they led her out of the room that had been her prison, through the Palace corridors and down to where the Royal Litter waited in readiness. This beautiful carriage, carved and inlaid with silver and gold, had been used in the past on many happy occasions. Now, looking at it anew, she shuddered and drew back; this morning, she felt as though it was taking her to her death. Then, as if sleepwalking, she climbed into it, and felt it being lifted by the men who would carry it all the way to Stonehenge. She tried the doors, but they were securely fastened. There was nothing she could do now to prevent her fate, save to hope that Boy, Merlin and Efflan would somehow be able to rescue her.

While Princess Guinevere was going through her own private agony, Whittle was marshalling the forces, tasked by Merlin, with her rescue. He had managed to assemble several hundred able-bodied volunteers, both men and women, who had gladly come to help their Princess in her peril. Most of them were ordinary folk, although there were also a number of Chieftains, other tribal leaders and trained fighting men among them.

Once assembled in the woods and given their orders, they formed into small groups and made their way, separately, towards Stonehenge; taking care to look inconspicuous and not attract attention. They were able to meet, and mass together again outside the building, without anyone becoming suspicious. Some did have small weapons, concealed in their garments, but, in a surprise assault, Merlin thought that hand-to-hand unarmed combat would be most effective. When the signal to attack came, their strategy would be to use brute force and overpower the enemy by sheer weight of numbers.

Inside, following its transformation into a temple to the Horned God Cernunnos, the Great Hall of Stonehenge was a dark, macabre and fearsome place. A circle of black-robed priests ringed the central area, singing the praises of Cernunnos and Modred with equal fervour. In the seat attached to the central pole, recently occupied by the reluctant Princess Guinevere, Prince Modred now sat, enthroned high above everyone, in all his baleful glory.

His madness had increased to such a point, that he now believed himself to be not merely a worshipper of Cernunnos, but so god-like as to be considered his equal. He wore a fantastic head-dress, which towered high above him and gave the impression that a pair of antlers, magnificent enough to rival those of the Horned God

257

himself, were growing out of his head, which was encircled by a heavy gold crown.

Seen in the flickering light from the huge candles and through the billowing smoke from the altar fire, he looked like some inhuman creature, half man and half beast. Around his neck was a finely-crafted gold torc, and he held another in his right hand, while his left hand grasped a rod of authority, shaped like a ram-headed serpent; symbols that echoed those carried by the huge idol behind him. Beside him, on a gold-embroidered cushion, sat his wart-encrusted Toad. This now wore a gold collar, with precious stones fastened to its back, where the sparkling jewels only emphasised its loathsome ugliness.

When the drums sounded, the Elders and members of the High Council began to file in through the main door. As they passed Modred's elevated throne, all had to bow low before him and then take their places, as part of the congregation. The priests had improvised a set of wooden steps, to allow Modred to descend in due course and graciously welcome his bride, but, for the moment, these had been set to one side, until her arrival. Meanwhile, he sat on high, in all his glory, revelling in his newly revealed god-like status.

Earlier, Merlin had once more given his guards the slip and silently entered Stonehenge unnoticed, through one of the side doors, which were impossible to find by those who did not know their secret location. Once inside, it was easy for him to move swiftly around in the shadows and unfasten each door in turn. Outside, Whittle and his men were poised, ready to burst in when the signal to attack was given.

In his full ceremonial robes and regalia as High Priest, Efflan stood waiting in the centre of the building, nervously hoping that Merlin's scheme would go according to plan and that he would survive the day. He was well aware that if anything went wrong, so that he could not perform the marriage ceremony, Modred would have him killed on the spot.

To Princess Guinevere, the journey from the Royal Palace to Stonehenge seemed to pass far too swiftly. She was heavily guarded, to prevent any attempts to free her en route, and her escort was under strict orders that she must arrive exactly on time at mid-day.

Modred waited impatiently, seated on his throne like a spider in the middle of its web – in his case a web of lies, deceit and death. Looking down on the assembled multitude with sneering contempt, he kept rubbing his hands together. 'Come in, come in, my little flies,' he chuckled to himself.

Then, the Royal Litter arrived, outside the main door into Stonehenge, exactly at noon, and the Princess Guinevere was reluctantly escorted into the building. She came to a standstill, just inside and looked about her. The appalling sight that met her eyes was, she thought, like a vision from Hell. Crowds of despairing souls huddled together, below a monstrous, devilish-looking figure, whose seated form towered over them through the smoke and flames rising from an altar dedicated to the fearsome Cernunnos. Catching sight of the antlers springing from his head, she thought, shuddering, 'Can that be a man or a beast?' Then it looked towards her and spoke: 'Welcome, my dear!' came the exalted words, and to her unspeakable horror, she realised that the dreadful being before her was Modred, himself, her self-styled husband-to-be.

The huge doors closed firmly behind her. On either side of her, the priests lined up, in two rows, and her escort forced her to walk slowly and reluctantly forward. As she approached the centre of the Great Hall, she was shaking with fear, feeling very small and very lonely. Then, leaning forward in his seat as she drew near, Modred declared loudly and boastfully: 'In my new, god-like form, I command your adoration and worship. Bow before me, and give the homage due to your future husband and King!'

In an instant, the full horror of her position suddenly dawned on Guinevere; it seemed that Merlin, and even Boy, had failed to save her, and she was on the brink of damnation. Losing all control, with her hands outstretched, she screamed, as loudly as she could!

At this high-pitched sound of terror, all the doors of Stonehenge suddenly burst open, as Whittle and his men charged into the building. Merlin's plan of a surprise attack worked perfectly; most of the guards were fortunately caught unawares still outside, and everything happened in seconds, as fierce hand-to-hand fighting broke out in the Great Hall! Seated above the turmoil, Modred saw that the attackers were, for the most part, overcoming his guards with their bare hands, and squealed loudly 'Kill them! Kill them all!'

It was at this moment that Boy, from his position high in the apex of the roof, grabbed the top of the central pole and prepared to descend. As he did so, he reached out to arm himself with Excalibur, but to his horror the handle slipped out of his grasp; despite a last-minute frantic lunge, he was unable to grab it again before gravity took over and he began his unstoppable slide downwards.

Modred had been so anxiously watching, as the fighting surged to and fro below him, that he was completely unaware of Boy's descent. Boy landed with a loud thump, on top of the throne's high back and kicked Modred hard, on the back of his head, dislodging his crown and antlered head-dress, which went crashing to the ground. Snarling in fury, Modred snatched a sharp dagger from his belt and tried to stab Boy in the legs. Boy kicked out again, then quickly grabbed Modred, by the wrist, and twisted it in an attempt to disarm him. Modred writhed and hissed curses, in anger that this upstart youth should dare attempt to thwart his desires.

So evil and twisted had his face become in his frenzy, and his eyes blazed in such rage, that Boy could hardly bear to look at him. The two of them were both struggling and hanging on to the seat while they continued fighting fiercely.

Seeing what was happening, all the other combatants froze at that moment and watched. Despite being hampered by his heavy robes and gold jewellery, Modred was bigger and stronger than Boy and was slowly beginning to overpower him. He seized the lad by the throat and leaned over him, pressing down heavily, with all his weight and strength.

Boy wriggled and struggled manfully, but Modred held him fast and he was powerless to resist. Modred lifted up his head and, with a wild glare in his eyes, shouted: 'See, I am truly divine; I am undefeatable!' Then he raised his dagger high in the air and prepared to deliver the fatal blow. Guinevere covered her eyes; she could look no more. 'It is horrible,' she cried inwardly, 'this is the end of everything; Modred has won!'

During all this time, the vibrations set up by the struggle had reached the top of the pole, and then, having shaken loose at that very moment, Excalibur fell. Silently, from the darkness, twisting and turning as it descended, the sword flew down, faster and faster, gathering speed as it travelled, until suddenly it struck! The blade hit Modred, with such force that it went straight through his body, piercing his black heart and pinning him to his throne. He had a single fraction of a second when he suddenly became aware of Excalibur, and he had just enough time to utter one last high-pitched, terrified shriek. So loud and full of agony was it, that everyone in the Great Hall covered their ears; this was the cry of a lost soul, aware it was about to descend into the everlasting torment of Hell.

Freeing himself from the grasp of Modred's bloodstained corpse, Boy climbed unsteadily down and left the body still firmly skewered to the seat. As the last of Modred's supporters fled from the building, hotly pursued by Whittle's men, he went over to where Princess Guinevere was still kneeling in shock. Exhausted beyond belief, he whispered 'Modred is dead! There is nothing to fear! His reign of terror has ended; everything is going to be alright!'

Chapter Twenty-six

It was as though the sun had broken through the clouds after a violent storm. Everyone suddenly felt a great sense of relief and liberty once again. The very air felt fresher and cleaner. Those falsely imprisoned by Modred's corrupt followers were released, and rejoined their families.

The good news spread throughout the kingdom like wildfire: 'The tyrant is dead! Modred has been killed; we are free again, free!' The days of rejoicing became weeks, and celebrations followed everywhere.

Once this natural outpouring of joy at the defeat and death of a monstrous tyrant had begun to calm down, the lengthy process of recovery started across the whole country. Everyone, from the Elders and members of the High Council to the lowliest labourer had been affected in some way by Modred's evil web of lies and dishonesty.

Those High Council members who had been seduced from their true allegiance quickly saw the error of their ways, and this mighty body was soon restored to its former state of integrity. Durrel, the Senior Elder who had remained incorruptibly loyal throughout, had to oversee a similar purging of his own colleagues, as did Brenon with his fellow-Chieftains. In the Royal Palace, Modred's lackeys had been expelled instantly, and Merlin had suggested that, as High Priest, Efflan would make an excellent father figure, to provide the still-traumatised Princess Guinevere with spiritual counselling, and to assist her in re-establishing order among members of the Royal Household.

Following his life-or-death combat with Modred, Boy had been cheered by all, and carried shoulder-high as a hero. At first he appeared to be his normal cheerful self, if incredibly weary after his efforts, but Merlin soon sensed that he was suffering greatly inside. The near-death experience to which he had been exposed had taken its toll, and his mind was still in revolt at the close contact he had been forced into with Modred's evil spirit.

Added to this Boy, like everyone else at that time, had been trained to believe that the taking of a human life was the ultimate taboo, no matter what the circumstances. So in addition to the emotional turmoil he was going through, Boy had strong feelings of guilt as being indirectly responsible for Modred's death.

Merlin knew that he had to act swiftly, so he spirited Boy away to a secret refuge where he would find peace, calm and relaxation. Merlin also helped the mental healing process with medicines made from herbs. Slowly Boy began to mend, and the terrible nightmare was finally put

266

behind him. His main worry now was the well-being of Guinevere, or "Grainne" as he still called her, but when Merlin reassured him that she was in safe keeping he smiled and relaxed. After several days, thanks to Merlin's herbal lore and skilled nursing, Boy was to all appearances his old self again and eager to play a part in the urgent work of reconstruction.

As soon as they had re-established their authority, the members of the High Council were faced with the task of weeding out Modred's followers from all the other places of power into which they had insinuated themselves. This would inevitably take time, as his slimy tentacles had spread far and wide.

A beginning was made with the tyrant's two leading lieutenants in infamy, Potter and Bullpin. Following Modred's death they had thrown away their weapons and fled, later to be discovered trying to make their escape in disguise. Now they were abject prisoners in the very dungeons where they had tormented so many of their innocent captives for so long.

At first the majority of High Council members were in favour of their immediate execution, but Merlin asked to address them in secret session to decide the pair's fate. He pointed out that such a death would be too mercifully quick; they had spent many long years abusing and torturing hundreds if not thousands of innocent men and women. A more fitting punishment, he suggested, would be for them to be kept in perpetual imprisonment. This found universal favour, and the decree was quickly passed with acclamation.

The sounds that could afterwards be heard coming from the deepest of the dungeons suggested that Potter and Bullpin were both being forced to make amends for their crimes the hard way!

Merlin knew well that the nation's establishment and the people at large all needed time to grieve over the loss of their greatly loved King and Queen, as well as to recover from the brief but immensely damaging period of Modred's power-crazed rule. All were still to some degree in a state of shock, and national recovery would inevitably be a lengthy process.

Meanwhile Merlin was already working in his own way to bring back an overall feeling of safety and stability within which people could work constructively and plan for the future.

'Wrongs do not, unfortunately, right themselves,' he thought. The nation would need all the help it could get.

There was, however, one immediate task he could undertake which would point the way. 'It will instantly help to re-establish people's pride and belief in themselves and their country,' he mused, 'if I arrange for Stonehenge to be re-consecrated, and by so doing, restore honour and pride to people's hearts.'

First, though, the great building had to be refurbished and restored to its former glory. All traces of Modred's insane alterations needed to be removed and destroyed. Merlin called all members of his former workforce together, and they gladly agreed to continue giving freely of their time until the great building was truly completed.

The next step was to visit Stonehenge, which had been kept empty and under guard since the dreadful day which had culminated in Modred's death. As soon as they entered, the entire group was struck with the sense of evil that still hung heavily overall. The candles and the altar fires had been extinguished, and the pure light of day pouring down through the apex now illuminated the Great Hall brilliantly, but all within seemed barren and tawdry. There was even a feeling that something horrible might still be moving in there, creeping about in the farthest distant dark corners. Although it was a warm day, many shivered involuntarily and looked around nervously.

Merlin saw that the only way to help them overcome their fears was to put them to work as quickly as possible, and rapidly ran through the details of what needed to be done. 'First of all,' he said loudly and confidently, 'will a group of you please remove that dreadful image of the Horned God? He has no power in this sacred place, and so cannot harm anyone. Take it outside and burn it, so that it can go back to where it came from; Cernunnos will then pursue and torment Modred's evil spirit forever!'

They approached it very cautiously, but once the fearsome idol had been pulled down and manhandled without mishap everyone grew bolder. And by the time it had been pulled down and carried outside the bearers had started laughing. Inside, Merlin said to those remaining, 'Will someone please remove that ugly set of steps, and Brad, will you take down and remove that ridiculous pole stretching to and from the apex? Then perhaps you, Reann, would be good enough to continue your beautifully skilful work on the symbol in the centre of the floor?'

Soon everyone began to join in, and all were glad to help in clearing away the remains of Modred's blasphemous trappings. While this was going on, one of the workers suddenly stopped and called to Merlin; hearing the note of fear in his voice, Merlin hurried across to find they had uncovered Modred's pet Toad, which had scuttled away in the confusion and hidden under some draperies. Their immediate instinct was to kill it, but Merlin explained that, loathsome though it might look, the creature itself had committed no crime and should therefore be spared.

He prised the jewels from its back, then arranged for the creature to be put into a basket and carried it himself deep into the countryside, away from human habitation. The moment Merlin released it, the gruesome creature crawled under a large stone and vanished down a hole. 'So,' mused Merlin, 'you have gone to join your master in the Otherworld!'

Back at Stonehenge, Brad was tasked with organising a team to make and fit the great seats that would be supported by the Blue Stones. They would only be supported at the back and not the front, thus giving the illusion that they were floating one foot above the ground. Each one of these great seats was to have a wooden canopy above it, elaborately carved and embossed with gold. This was just one of many additions to the splendour, majesty and mystery of Stonehenge.

Where the main structure of the building was concerned, Merlin had planned that a second set of doors would be hung. This was so that whenever people entered Stonehenge the main doors would close behind them before the inner doors opened, creating a sense of anticipation. In this way, those entering the building for the first time would have no idea of the spectacle they were about to encounter, making the impact all the stronger when the inner doors were finally opened. To increase this

271

feeling of wonderment, the doors would be opened and shut without making a sound by means of a carefully hidden rope and pulley, giving the impression that they were operating of their own accord – as if by magic.

At the same time, finishing touches were made to the floor, with wood colourants and stains being applied so as to create a wonderful pattern and enhance the beauty of the carefully-selected timber which had been used in its construction. In fact everything in the interior of Stonehenge was constructed using the finest craftsmanship, with the many carvings being designed to look superb, yet not over-ornate.

The whole feeling and atmosphere of this restored interior was now one of quality and balance, strength and subtlety. Around the centre were the seven great seats, for the use of the King, the High Priest, the Senior Member of the High Council, the Senior Elder and a representative from each of the disciplines of education, law and medicine. There was also an outer circle of sixteen seats, set out equally, some for members of the public, others for witnesses and recorders.

The main function of this layout was to create a sense of fairness, honesty, honour and truth. People would feel that they could place complete trust in such a learned and experienced body of men and women, and know for certain that their decisions would be strictly impartial, not ruled by self-interest. Stonehenge would be the place where people could come for trial or judgement, or to have disputes settled; even to undergo reconciliation or healing in certain cases.

It was also a building designed to impress; for example, foreign dignitaries who entered would indeed feel that they were dealing with a major power, a country capable of great things.

Chapter Twenty-seven

The cleansing and refurbishment of the interior of Stonehenge continued apace, whilst Merlin involved himself in organising the final touches to be made to the main structure. Before coming to the Isle of Breton, in a land far away he had studied the secrets of making glass, a material totally unknown to anyone except King Arthur, to whom, at the beginning of their friendship, he had given the crystal ball. Also, early on in the planning of Stonehenge, Merlin had worked with Old Sniffy, the acknowledged furnace-master; having first sworn him to secrecy, and explained to him the complex procedures of how to make glass from different compounds.

Finally it was time to start the most difficult stage of the construction, which would involve glass-making on a grand scale. Old Sniffy had for several months been building furnaces hot enough to enable him to produce small quantities of clear glass, which he and his assistants had stored in sacks and hidden, well away from prying eyes. They now had sufficient glass to allow them to begin the moulding process.

It was at this difficult stage that Merlin decided to ask Boy, as his trusted apprentice, if he would assist them.

Eager to play an active part in things, Boy agreed without hesitation.

Before he would let him begin, however, Merlin warned him as he had warned Old Sniffy, that: 'The work we are doing here is one of the most important secrets of Stonehenge. You must swear to keep secret everything you see and do, and make absolutely certain that you never tell anyone, not even your own family!'

With all involved sworn to secrecy, the three of them set to and began working as a team. First of all, with a great deal of hard labour, together they built a huge furnace, bigger than anything else anyone had previously seen. It was set in an isolated hillside, with the tunnel running up to the top of the hill to create a strong draught on the main fire. Once lit, the furnace would have to become very hot indeed in order to maintain the very high temperatures necessary for the long process of moulding.

Old Sniffy took his craftsman's skills to the limit, achieving a furnace bigger and better than anything ever seen before. This was Old Sniffy at his best; he became alive with enthusiasm, revelling in the preparations and enjoying every minute with relish. The furnace area was covered over to keep the heat in; this covering was made of stone and clay baked very hard to hold the intense heat without any danger of cracking.

What they intended to make were a number of large triangular plates of glass by means of a process which Merlin referred to as "Cascade". This method proposed that the glass would flow out of the furnace, cascade down a triangular slipway, and spread out into a large triangular sheet of glass.

On the appointed day Old Sniffy brought the furnace up to the correct temperature, then his assistants emptied all the small pieces of glass into the furnace. After giving all the pieces sufficient time to melt, Old Sniffy called out to Boy, who promptly unplugged the now molten glass so that it started to flow down the slipway. As it did so, Merlin demonstrated to the two of them how to hold back the glass, allowing it to spread equally over the long triangular slope so that it covered the whole area evenly.

This proved a very complex procedure, which even Merlin was unable to get exactly right the first time he attempted it, since the temperature and viscosity of the glass, coupled with the angle of the slipway, were all critical to a successful outcome of the process.

It took many trials and inevitable errors to begin with, but eventually both Old Sniffy and Boy grew sufficiently skilled to master the process, and between them they managed to produce no fewer than ten identical sheets of clear glass. This did not happen overnight; it took more than two months of hard work to complete the task. Nevertheless when Merlin saw what they had achieved he was overjoyed.

'Aha!' he exclaimed, 'now at last I can reveal why we have gone to all the time and trouble to make these "windows" as I call them.'

Merlin went on to explain, 'There are ten sheets, because they are designed to fit exactly into the apex of Stonehenge! That's why they have been made to precise measurements. When you are actually inside Stonehenge and looking up at the opening in the roof you would never know they were there, as it is too high to see anything different from the ground. The light will pass through, but it stops the rain.'

Boy was amazed to realise that this gave a whole extra dimension to the Great Hall. Struggling to come to terms with something so outside his usual mental horizons, even after absorbing all the things he had been taught by Merlin, he exclaimed, 'You both knew all along and did not tell me!' Merlin smiled. 'This is amazing,' Boy went on, 'no one will ever be able to work out what has been done.'

Then looking straight at Merlin, he asked him, 'This is the most important part of Stonehenge, isn't it?' The old man replied, still smiling, 'There is one more final piece to the jigsaw, but you will have to wait until the time arrives when all the right people are together, before I will reveal any further explanation of what is to come.'

All of which left Boy in a perfect frenzy of eager curiosity which he had perforce to control as best he could, since Merlin would not utter a further word on the matter.

Not long afterwards Merlin calculated that the time was now right to reveal this last and most important secret of Stonehenge. He therefore arranged a secret meeting of his carefully chosen people, inviting Princess Guinevere, Efflan, Durrel, Brenon, Reann, Brad, Magnus, Old Sniffy and Boy, who by now was almost bursting with curiosity. Each one was invited individually, so that no one knew who else would be present, or had any idea of what to expect. Their meeting-place, the location of which was not divulged to another soul, was a large circular hut at the edge of the high plain.

Inside the hut was a single lamp illuminating a set of trestles; apart from that, the place was empty. Merlin stepped forward and asked all those present to remain in the shadows and wait patiently without saying a word. All was silent as the minutes passed. After what seemed like quite a long time there was a single tap on the double doors. Merlin opened them, and then four men carrying a stretcher entered the room. They placed this across the trestles, then left without a word being spoken.

Everyone looked at the stretcher with the greatest interest; on it was a large oblong object wrapped in old sacking. Merlin deftly lifted this outer covering and revealed a plain wooden chest, which he said contained something very special. Opening the lid, he gestured to Boy to help him lift out whatever was inside. Even now, no one could make out what it was, as it had been carefully wrapped for protection in a quantity of fine linen. Consumed with curiosity, all those present moved forward to get a better view as Merlin carefully unwrapped the linen, fold by fold.

Everyone gasped in amazement as it was finally revealed: a gigantic and extremely beautiful Crystal, which shone like a magical jewel as the lamplight refracted inside it and reflected back into the room. The Crystal was huge, almost two feet across, and had been made to a very complex design. Exquisite in itself, it was shining, absolutely aglow with light as they all silently came closer to gather round it, no one said a word as they looked at this totally unexpected apparition. Merlin looked around to see their faces lit up by the Crystal, which had rendered them all speechless. It was by far the most beautiful object any of them had ever seen.

Chapter Twenty-eight

All those chosen to view the Crystal could hardly find words to express their amazement at its beauty and size. Eventually Princess Guinevere gasped, 'It's...it's the most beautiful jewel I've ever seen; it must be the biggest in the whole world!' Even rugged Reann, always the most stern of women, could be seen to smile as she gazed into its glorious depths.

Boy, as usual, was thinking hard. 'There can be nothing else in existence like it,' he said, 'but however amazing the Crystal is, surely it can't be just a beautiful object. You must have a planned use for it, Merlin, haven't you?'

'Right as usual, Boy,' replied Merlin, 'it is the most important secret of Stonehenge. It will reflect and direct the light from the sun and all the colours of the rainbow, which will appear inside the building.'

'Look closely at it,' he went on, 'there are reasons for the shape in which it is fashioned. The Crystal is made to precise measurements and angles that are related to the Summer and Winter Solstices, also the Spring and Autumn Equinoxes. It is in alignment with the heavens, so that the reflections it casts will create signs and symbols, all of which have different meanings.

'These can be interpreted as signs from the Gods. They will appear in different places at different times. No one will be like any other; they will be seen, and therefore we will be affected by their appearance. Stonehenge will not be an inert, empty building but the light will change constantly and therefore create theatre and drama as the interior brightens or darkens with changes in the weather. When the sun appears from behind a cloud, polarised light will shine down, thus transforming the atmosphere within the building itself.'

Princess Guinevere gasped in wonder as she imagined how this magical light would look, shining down from above. Merlin smiled and continued, 'Also, the dimensions of the Crystal are linked to the symbol in the centre of the floor; in fact everything at Stonehenge is interconnected.'

When he had finished speaking, Efflan the High Priest clasped his hands together and declared. 'When this most sacred object has been placed in position as the crowning glory of Stonehenge I shall declare a Day of Consecration to give thanks to the Gods for this mighty and most precious gift!'

Work was soon under way to turn this amazing vision into reality. As the secret of the apex was still unknown to all but the selected few whom Merlin had confided in, the task of setting the Crystal into place was undertaken by

Brad and Boy, who worked together in secret. In order to reach the apex, they built a temporary wooden scaffold. Brad worked from this platform, while Boy did all the fetching and carrying.

At the apex the wooden beams had all been cut to exactly the same length, to act as a secure setting for the Crystal. This had been made to fit precisely into the top of the apex, so that it would appear to anyone looking upwards that the beams holding up the roof simply ended in mid-air. All that was visible from inside Stonehenge would be the sky, as if nothing at all was holding up the centre of the roof.

It took over two weeks to fit the Crystal tightly and securely in place, then Brad cut special recesses in the beams for the windows to be fitted. One of the most difficult and dangerous operations was lifting the enormous triangular pates of glass up the long sloping side of the roof. One slip would have meant disaster. The Gods were kind, however; all went well, and when Brad and Boy had managed to fit and seal all the windows, the building of Stonehenge was finally complete.

Except for the small group of people carefully chosen by Merlin to be involved in the building operations, no one else knew anything about the Crystal itself or the ten glass windows. They would still see the sky and the sunlight shining down through the great opening in the apex of the roof, but so expertly had the final additions been made that they would never be able to guess that there was now a protective layer between them and the elements above.

The secrets of the Crystal, and how it worked in relation to the sun, were beyond most people's understanding. Only Merlin had known in advance how the colours would refract, and just how magnificent all the light would appear.

Once Stonehenge had been completed, Merlin had arranged with Efflan for it to be closed to the people until a suitable great occasion presented itself for the building's consecration and inauguration. In the meantime, he spent long hours in the building alone, taking measurements and readings from reflections at different times. He would often remain there all day, and sometimes throughout the night. Occasionally, he would discuss his deductions and calculations with Efflan, who as High Priest had a special interest in how these might affect the interpretation of his own readings of the heavens. Mostly, however, during this special time of research, Merlin was a man who preferred to work alone.

With all the building work completed, and Merlin preoccupied in deep matters beyond the comprehension of all others, Boy was at something of a loose end. His thoughts and dreams now centred on Princess Guinevere, and while it would not have been at all correct, according to royal protocol, for him to visit her alone, he managed to meet and talk with her on several occasions when other people were also present.

Sometimes they were actually able to slip away together for short periods, as when Guinevere took him to see the 'house' – the scale model of Stonehenge – that Merlin had given her. Since then she had made it even more beautiful by furnishing it with great taste and style – furniture, wall hangings and ornaments had all been chosen to set it off to perfection.

Boy was enchanted by it and as they stood together, for once alone and holding hands, he said shyly, 'This house is now a part of you, Grainne – for so I shall always think of you. I can see all the love and thought you have put into it. The Royal Palace is certainly very grand, but this is your home. I fear I have nothing to give you, except my love and a few small flowers.' Tenderly he handed her the posy he was carrying, picked that morning, and continued, 'You know I meant it that time when I said I loved you?'

Guinevere lowered her long, fair eyelashes and blushed, while unseen between them her hand tightened its grip on Boy's. Then very softly but clearly she replied, 'Yes, Boy, I also love you.' He almost shouted for joy, then put his arms

285

around her and held her closely. They kissed and held each other, gazing silently and happily into each other's eyes.

In the world at large, life was gradually settling down again after the trauma of King Arthur's murder and the terrors of Modred's brief, insane usurpation of power. Soon, however, another major event in their history began to excite the people's attention.

With the functions of the Elders and the High Council restored to normal, the lack of a reigning monarch began to make itself keenly felt. Both bodies began to discuss the question of a possible successor to the late King.

Various queries immediately presented themselves. Would it be acceptable, for example, for Princess Guinevere to become Queen in her own right? Who would be the next in line to the throne? These and other topics were debated at great length, but without much subsequent action being taken. Another suggestion was to have an elected Monarchy, decided by all the Chieftains representing all areas, with a new King being chosen from a list of suitable candidates.

Others accepted that the country could survive with a female ruler who was Queen in her own right, but pointed out that if she married it would mean her husband, although having the title of King, would always be in a secondary position – and that would never do! Alternatively, could they find a King through birthright? Many believed that a true King would emerge by his strength of will or natural leadership. On one thing all were agreed; it was essential for the country as a whole that a new King should be found. But who would be the next King? And who would come up with the right answer?

Chapter Twenty-nine

Never before, in the long history of the Isle of Breton had there been a need to elect a new Monarch. In normal circumstances, the King would have named his successor prior to his death. Possibly a member of the Royal Family or a strong, wise leader would have been the obvious candidate. It was the King who always decided, so there was therefore no precedent for the process of selection that now faced the great and the good.

There was much debate on how they should go about making their choice. Eventually Merlin, Efflan and Durrel agreed that a special meeting should be held and attended only by those who were very senior and high ranking. These comprised, besides the three already named, Princess Guinevere as the sole surviving member of the Royal Family, all the Elders and members of the High Council, and the most senior Chieftains. They would be present as representatives of all the people, to speak on their behalf.

When all were assembled, Merlin as master of ceremonies called upon Brenon to open the meeting. The former High Chieftain had been promoted following the removal of all Modred's henchmen from positions of power, and had been the unanimous choice to become the new Head of the High Council. Now he was to be the main speaker on this momentous occasion, the outcome of which would affect the future of the Kingdom for many years ahead. Merlin had discussed matters with him beforehand, and they had agreed a form of procedure suitable for such an important meeting.

Rising to his feet, Brenon began solemnly, 'We are here today to choose a new King. Yet no obvious choice presents itself, and we have to decide what is best to be done. Is there anyone among us here who could take the place of our late Lord and Sovereign King Arthur?'

All eyes were on Princess Guinevere as he finished speaking; although a Queen had never ruled the country in her own right before, the Princess was every inch her father's daughter, and admired for being a spirited girl with a mind of her own. But knowing the role was beyond her powers, she just shook her head sadly and said nothing.

Somewhat disappointed, Brenon shrugged his shoulders and went on to ask his next question, 'Will anyone step forward to propose some other candidate?' no one moved; there was a long silence while everyone waited for someone else to make a suggestion.

As High Priest, it was Efflan's turn to rise and speak next.

'If the temporal power is unable to solve our pressing dilemma,' he said, 'we must invoke the spiritual power and turn to the Gods! Whom would they have chosen? Better still – whom have they already chosen? For they know what will come to pass, and though we have been ignorant of their decision, I believe that here in this room today the answer will be revealed to us!'

As he spoke with increasing passion and conviction, a change came over the old man. His voice became stronger and louder, easily reaching the farthest corners of the room, and he brandished his staff with all the vigour of someone much younger. It was as though he was possessed by a higher power which was speaking through him.

'King Arthur was a man of faith,' he continued, 'it was his destiny, along with Merlin, to preside over the building of Stonehenge, a place where men and Gods can come together. I believe this very coming together is occurring as I speak! I ask you all, who knows more about Stonehenge than anyone else? Who was involved in its construction right from the beginning? Who has spent most of his life working on Stonehenge? Who showed his courage and resolution in rescuing our Princess and restoring our mighty building to the true faith by bringing about the death of the evil tyrant Modred? The Gods did not even give him a name, because I believe he is destined to be the next King

Arthur! Most of you have seen him; many of you know him or have heard of him. He is called only – Boy!'

There was a sharp intake of breath from all present, which could clearly be heard echoing round the room as Efflan resumed his seat. It was not a gasp of surprise or incredulity, but of relief. There had been so much conviction and authority in Efflan's voice that all present felt he had indeed been inspired to speak by the Gods.

Many said afterwards that it was as if a mighty rushing wind had passed through the room, leaving them clear-headed and with an absolute sense of certainty that Efflan was right. He had truly been an ambassador of the Gods, to speak on their behalf. No one needed any further convincing; in fact after a very short pause Efflan realised that all present had risen to their feet as one man, and were loudly cheering his words!

Raising his hands for silence, Efflan waited until the applause had quietened down. He began to speak again.

'Who, then,' he asked, 'will be the one to tell him of our decision?'

Many people looked around at their neighbours, but did not utter a word. None felt themselves worthy to undertake such a momentous task.

Then Princess Guinevere rose to her feet and declared in a strong, clear voice, 'I know of only one man here who deserves that right. It must be – Merlin!'

Everyone cheered again!

Then Merlin himself stood up before them all and spoke, saying, 'Who can question the wisdom of the Gods? It was all meant to be; the Gods have chosen us all. We are their people and now, with their guidance, we have chosen a King. By your leave, I will set out straight away to find him. When the time is right we will come together again, but next time it will be in the presence of our new King – Arthur!'

Finally Brenon rose to his feet and said in a loud voice, 'The King is dead; long live the King!' and everyone cheered a third time!

Merlin bowed to the assembly, turned and walked slowly from the meeting room alone. He had much to think about now, but was in no hurry; the great decision had been taken. Following his instinct, he walked over the high plain towards the edge of the escarpment. Soon he saw in the distance two seated figures who looked familiar, and as he neared them he recognised both Boy and his father Whittle.

It was Whittle who saw him first and called out, 'Merlin! What brings you here this evening?'

'I have come to see Boy,' the old man replied.

Sensing the visit was important Whittle rose, stretched himself and took his leave.

When Whittle had gone, Merlin said 'Don't get up.' Boy remained seated on the rock from whence he had been looking out over the lower levels into the far distance.

'What are you really doing here, Merlin?' Boy asked curiously.

'Oh, I'm just out for a stroll,' he replied casually, with a smile.

They sat together looking at the view and watching the sun slowly descend.

Eventually Merlin said, 'This is where it all began. Do you know how long it has been since we started work on Stonehenge?'

In a low voice, Boy started to recall the various stages, 'Finding the Sarsen Stones, working out the route, seeing the Stoneroller in action, removing the soil from inside the building, and all the other problems we had to overcome.'

Merlin nodded and said, 'It was all part of the Gods' plan for us. Are you happy to have been part of it?'

Boy thought for a moment, then replied simply, 'It's part of me now; it's who I am.'

Merlin was silent for a while, then began somewhat hesitantly, 'There is no easy way to tell you this, I fear.'

Alarmed, Boy asked quickly, 'What is it, Merlin? Is something wrong?'

'With King Arthur dead,' the old man said solemnly, 'the country needs a new King. Boy, you are a boy no longer, you are a man. The Gods chose you to work on Stonehenge. Now – and believe me when I tell you this – they have chosen you to be our next King! Your name shall be Arthur, and you will be our future Monarch! To mark the occasion, I present you with this ring of pure gold; it is set with a precious stone, cut in the shape of the Crystal. Keep it safe, for you will have need of it one day!'

Boy looked at Merlin dumbfounded. He took the ring, but did not speak; he could find no words. They sat there for a long time as darkness fell, closer than they had ever been, yet with everything now changed between them.

Then Boy finally said in a small, hesitant voice, 'Who else knows about this?'

Merlin replied, 'Princess Guinevere, Efflan, Durrel and the Elders, Brenon and the High Council, and some of the High Chieftains. They were all at a very special meeting which was held today before I came to see you here.'

Boy shook his head as if in disbelief, then said quietly, 'Merlin, I was totally unprepared for this. I will need time to adjust and get used to the idea.'

'That's fine,' replied Merlin soothingly, 'that's just fine. We all need time to adjust!' They held each other in a hug, then Merlin said, 'You had better break the news to your Father yourself; I will come with you.'

Rising to their feet, they set off, walking slowly towards the village in the pale moonlit night.

Chapter Thirty

The next morning Boy, his head still whirling after Merlin's astonishing news, talked it all through again with his parents. Everything was strange; it was as if they were discussing something that had happened to another family.

Once he had got over his initial disbelief, however, Whittle felt immensely proud of the honour that had so suddenly descended on his son, yet humble in the knowledge that the Gods had looked kindly on his family above all others.

His wife Jenny's immediate reaction was to burst into tears; the whole thing was too much for her to take in, and she had an instinctive feeling that their family life in its present form would be at an end forever. Both husband and son took great pains to calm her down and reassure her that not all change was for the worse; she, too, should be proud of her boy at this time. Eventually she dried her eyes and a smile began to play about her lips as she thought of all the good things the future would hold.

Leaving his parents to adjust to their new status as best they could, Boy knew that the first thing he wanted to do was to visit Princess Guinevere. When he reached the Royal Palace all the guards stood to attention, while all the servants bowed low as he passed by. Merlin had seen to it that everyone in the Palace had been informed of the decision taken at the meeting, and that Boy was now the successor to the throne.

Acknowledging the salutes and bows as best he could, Boy proceeded directly to Princess Guinevere's apartments. No one questioned him as he knocked on her door. She opened it herself, exclaiming joyfully, 'Boy! I'm so glad it's you; how are you feeling after Merlin's great news?'

Thoughtfully he replied, 'Different. I don't know quite how, but different.'

He then suggested that they should go down to the "house" that Merlin had given her, and spend some time together alone.

Once inside the building, Boy slumped down in a seat with a very sad look on his face. Guinevere felt a twinge of alarm.

'What is it, Boy?' she asked, 'are you feeling unwell?'

'No, Grainne,' replied Boy in a low, despondent voice, 'not unwell, but unhappy. I feel I just cannot accept this great honour that has come to me. I am not worthy, whatever the Gods may have decided; I was content as I was, and do not have the knowledge or the skill to try to be what I am not. Grainne! Oh Grainne, I am so afraid!'

Hiding his head in his hands, he burst into deep sobs of anguish that shook his whole body.

Guinevere was beside him in a flash, cradling him in her arms and holding him close. 'Oh my dearest Boy,' she murmured, 'it must be hard for you, so hard! But no one can refuse what the Gods have given. It is part of their plan for us all. You are brave and strong, and you are always eager to learn. Of course you know nothing of the arts of Kingship, but remember I am my royal father's daughter; I learned much from him by looking and listening, and asking questions. I can help you! Together we will look after our country's welfare, and care for all the people in it.'

'You are always so wonderful, Grainne,' said Boy admiringly, 'but even with your help, I feel it will be beyond me.'

'Remember, Boy,' she replied, 'that you will not have to face the future alone. Merlin, of course, will counsel you, and there's Efflan and Durrel and Brenon and – oh so many people to guide you on your way! Each of us thinks he or she is alone, but help is always at hand. And it's not just people; when we're at our lowest ebb and we think we're completely powerless, as I was in Modred's evil clutches, there's a higher power on which we can always call. Think of when Excalibur fell! Boy, you are under the Gods' protection and must obey their decisions!'

'You are right as usual, Grainne,' said Boy quietly. 'I feel so ashamed; I have let you and everyone down, haven't I?'

'Nonsense,' replied Guinevere firmly, 'you haven't let anyone down. Of course you are scared of the future; anyone would be in your situation. So am I, if it comes to that! But we shall overcome all these difficulties; one day soon we will laugh at how timid we were!'

So the young couple kissed and promised to share their concerns with each other in future. When they returned to the Palace, they found Durrel and Efflan waiting for them. The pair had already begun plans for their new King's Coronation, Efflan explaining to Durrel that as a young man, newly chosen as High Priest, he had officiated when the first King Arthur was crowned. Despite his advancing years, he still remembered every detail of the ceremony, the origins of which went back long before the country's recorded history.

It had already been decided that Stonehenge was the obvious venue for this great ceremony. The new King would need to be suitably adorned, so special ceremonial clothing and royal robes had to be made. Both Efflan and Durrel were determined that their new ruler should be the first to enter the newly refurbished building, and that his appearance should be worthy of such a momentous occasion.

For this once in a lifetime event, seemingly endless preparations had to be made. Everyone was involved: Elders, the High Council, members of the palace staff and many more, all were kept busy and worked very hard to make sure that everything would be ready in time for the great day.

Although time did not allow invitations to be sent overseas to foreign royalty, messengers were sent out to every part of the country, proclaiming that all who could be present would be made welcome, with food and shelter provided.

For weeks beforehand the scene was one of constant activity, with everyone hurrying about their various tasks, and a seemingly endless selection of provisions being stockpiled in bewildering variety, not forgetting the vast quantities of mead required to wash it all down!

By this time Whittle and his wife Jenny, together with little Rosy and the other children, had been provided with temporary apartments in the Royal Palace, as befitted the new King's family. They were all rather overawed by their new lifestyle, and amid the bustle and grandeur of the Coronation preparations, they found themselves somewhat at a loss as to what was expected of them.

Fortunately Princess Guinevere had inherited her mother's talent for organisation, and she was beginning to take the royal household firmly in hand. No one was forgotten, and even at such a hectic time she made sure that someone was personally on hand to help Boy's parents prepare, and to guide them through all the formalities.

At the Coronation itself there would be parades and processions, together with a great deal of feasting and entertainment. All the people who had worked with Boy at Stonehenge had been specially invited to take part in the main procession; the strong Norseman Magnus in particular had made a banner to carry which was so huge and heavy that no one else could even lift it. The climax of the great day was to be a magnificent Coronation Banquet, catering for everyone's needs, all laid out on long tables inside a series of buildings not far from Stonehenge itself.

At last the great day of the Coronation arrived, and to everyone's relief it proved to be fine, warm and sunny. Boy had risen early, and stood patiently while his attendants bustled around helping him to dress and making sure that his kingly robes fitted and hung correctly. He was then escorted outside the Palace, and he walked, bareheaded, in procession to the beginning of the Royal Approach. From there he could see Stonehenge powerful and majestic in the distance, silhouetted on the horizon. He was still scarcely able to believe that he was not dreaming.

Then after a quick glance behind him, he started to walk down the gentle slope. Behind him came Princess Guinevere, transformed now from a headstrong girl into a very stately and regal young lady, dazzling in silver and gold. With her were her Royal relatives, Boy's family, all the Elders, members of the High Council and every Chieftain in the land.

It was a magnificent spectacle, applauded by the huge crowds, numbering thousands, who were lined up on the right-hand side of the procession. They had travelled many miles, some from the far corners of the land, to be present on this very special day, all hoping to get a glimpse of their new King. Nor were they disappointed; seeing them looking so happy and excited, Boy stopped for a moment, halting the whole procession, then turned and waved to them all. The whole crowd cheered again and again, and waved ecstatically back.

Boy walked slowly on again, up the Processional Avenue towards the outer circle. Then saw Merlin standing alone at the main doors, waiting to welcome his friend into Stonehenge. Merlin bowed reverently as Boy approached, then their hands clasped firmly as they met. They remained still and silent for a few moments amid the cheering multitude, then Boy walked inside the great building alone.

As the great doors closed behind him, he stood before the second set of doors and gently opened them. The spectacle that confronted him made him blink his eyes in wonder; he just could not believe what he was seeing.

The whole interior of Stonehenge was filled with a strong, beautiful light, all sparkling and glistening. He stepped forward, and stood directly in the centre. Here he felt transfigured, aglow in the flood of polarised light which the sun, now directly above the apex, was causing to emanate down from the Crystal.

Relaxing in the warmth of the sun's radiance, Boy looked around him, convinced that everything was perfect, just perfect. He admired in particular the floor with its striking, star-shaped central symbol, polished and inlaid so beautifully, with the seats around it so big and grand. At this moment, while still quite alone, he fell to his knees and prayed silently.

The doors then opened to admit Merlin, who walked up as Boy rose to his feet again and stood beside him. To fanfares of horns, the remainder of the great procession, led by Princess Guinevere, now entered into the Great Hall of Stonehenge and took their appointed places. There was a short pause, then Efflan, robed in gleaming white garments, entered through a different door. In procession followed his assistant priests, who grouped themselves about him, while he stood alone in the glorious light.

Raising his arms, Efflan declared, 'You are all welcome here today, on this great occasion. Our new King, Arthur who was Boy, is to be crowned in the presence of you all, but first we need a sign from the Gods!'

The sun, which had disappeared behind clouds for a while, burst out again, and the building was once more flooded with radiant light.

'The Gods have answered us!' cried Efflan triumphantly, 'It is time for the Coronation to begin!'

More priests now entered in procession, one at the head carrying Excalibur, and another bearing the Royal Crown on a beautifully embroidered cushion. Efflan motioned Boy to approach where he stood in the centre, and to kneel before him.

Raising his arms once again, he began to proclaim, 'On this day, in this sacred place of Stonehenge and before all who are gathered here,' then he paused, took Excalibur and continued, 'I name you Arthur,' touching Boy on each shoulder with the sword.

After this he handed it to him, then turned and took the Crown, raised the gem-studded gold diadem high before all the people, then slowly placed it on Boy's head, saying, 'I now crown you King of the Isle of Breton. Arise, King Arthur!'

Following this, the new King Arthur was shown to the Royal Throne, and took his seat upon it. All present then filed past in order of precedence to bow and give homage, honour and respect to their King and Royal Sovereign.

When the ceremony was over, King Arthur walked slowly out of Stonehenge, still wearing his crown, to show himself to the people. As he appeared, the waiting crowd cheered loudly and long. Arthur – Boy no longer – climbed onto a small hillock so that he could see and be seen by all. Waving in greeting, he drew Excalibur and brandished it high in the air. This was greeted with more cheering again and again. After that he began to move among his people, so that everyone within reach had a chance to touch his Royal person, an act believed to be a sure way of staying healthy and happy.

Everyone was blissfully happy to be part of such a glorious day. The celebrations continued until all were well fed, mellow, and contented to return home once more, with never-to-be-forgotten memories of a truly historic and wonderful occasion.

King Arthur now took up permanent residence in the Royal Palace, while Merlin, Efflan, Durrel and the entire Royal Household continued to work unceasingly to build a structure of living that would be ideal for the new monarch and everyone concerned with the running of the country.

Arthur had been crowned King, but he still had to learn how to rule his Kingdom. In a sometimes hostile world, it was vital to ensure that the Isle of Breton was seen by all to be well governed, well defended and prosperous.

Chapter Thirty-one

With the Coronation now over, it took some considerable time for Arthur, as he now was, to adjust to his new role as King. The position of sole and ultimate responsibility proved at first to be a lonely and often frightening one. Even with the loving help of Guinevere, and the wise counsel of Merlin, Efflan and Durrel, it was not easy for him to begin with, but his natural curiosity enabled him to learn quickly.

One of the first things Merlin advised him to do was to undertake a Royal Tour of the country.

'It is most important, Sire,' he pointed out, 'that everyone should not only know that they have a new King, but also have the opportunity of seeing you. The advantage for national morale is very great, and will establish an understanding between you and your people. Later, it will be prudent for us to arrange a special occasion to which we can invite foreign royalty and dignitaries from all nations. They will be able to meet you in an atmosphere of ceremony and feasting during which new, friendly and hopefully mutually beneficial relationships can be forged.'

Durrel knew that a mixture of pageantry, display and celebrations was the ideal way for the new King Arthur to become popular. The lonely, daily grind of ruling would come later, when he was used to appearing in public, and more comfortable with his new life. Adoring, cheering crowds would not only boost national morale, but were also guaranteed to lift the spirits of even the most nervous new Monarch.

And so it proved. The Royal Tour, during which every corner of the land was visited, was a triumphant progress. King Arthur's natural, openly friendly manner proved to be a great asset, and he quickly established himself as a great favourite with all, not least the young ladies who delighted in deluging him with flowers whenever he walked among them.

This round of public engagements was carefully combined with a gradual introduction to the theory and practice of Kingship. There was so much that Arthur had to learn, including the day-to-day study of protocol and formalities. He would have to become familiar with every aspect of the law of the land, and become skilled in diplomatic negotiations with foreign powers, so Durrel had to ensure that Arthur was not overwhelmed by the complexity of it all.

After almost a year of induction and preparation, King Arthur felt ready to take personal command of his realm, and his advisors agreed. He began, therefore, by calling his Ministers, Elders and High Council together, to discuss the future of Stonehenge and his Royal Court. While they were engrossed in debating these matters and working out the details, Arthur himself slipped unobtrusively out of the Royal Council Chamber, and went to see Princess Guinevere.

They had been meeting as often as his training for royal duties would allow, spending time together relaxing and doing ordinary, everyday things like walking, riding and hunting. Then they would retire to what Guinevere now called 'their special house' and sit together laughing and talking for hours at a time.

On this particular day, everything proved so perfect that they did not want it to end. As evening came on, Arthur suddenly took Guinevere in his arms and said 'I love you, my dearest Grainne; You are so beautiful, I want to be with you always!' He then got down on one knee and asked her 'Will you marry me?'

'Oh, yes!' she replied joyfully, 'Arthur, I will marry you. I love you, too; I have dreamed of this day – I am so happy!'

Arthur then reached into the small leather bag hanging round his neck, and pulled out a folded cloth of fine linen. Unwrapping it carefully, he produced the beautiful gold ring that Merlin had given him when telling him of his great destiny. The precious stone set within this ring had been fashioned to be an exact miniature of the Crystal in the apex of Stonehenge. It glittered as he placed the ring on Guinevere's finger. It was a perfect fit! They kissed and embraced, declaring their true and everlasting love for each other.

Next day, Arthur hastened to tell Merlin and Efflan that he and Princess Guinevere were engaged. 'Just as I hoped!' thought Merlin joyfully to himself. Indeed the news came as no real surprise to either of them; they had been rather hoping that things would work out in precisely that way.

Once the wonderful news was announced, it generated an atmosphere of great excitement throughout the Palace. Then as the glad tidings spread further, the happy Royal couple had to make haste to tell Arthur's parents of their joyful news in person. Whittle and Jenny were overjoyed beyond measure, while young Rosy was both extremely happy and very excited at the prospect of being a Royal bridesmaid.

Good news travels fast, so it did not take long for the excitement to reach every corner of the country. Thousands upon thousands of people had already heard of Arthur, their brave new King, who had brought about the death of the evil Modred. Large numbers had seen him on his first

Royal Tour, and they knew, too, of the beautiful Princess Guinevere.

Many had travelled to see the Coronation; so who then could blame them for also wanting to be at the Royal Wedding? Additionally, the wedding could be utilised as the occasion of which Durrel had spoken, when he stressed the importance of Arthur's establishing good relations with foreign rulers. All the Royal Families throughout the world would be invited. The very best in entertainment would be provided for the happy occasion, with pageants, parades, music, dancing, feasting and celebrations which would last for many days.

As High Priest, Efflan was consulted as to what date would be propitious, and he declared that the Royal Wedding should be held on the Spring Equinox. There followed an instant bustle of preparation; invitations had to be sent out in large numbers both at home and abroad; the feasts and entertainments had to be planned and prepared; banners, decorations and dresses had to be made.

Stonehenge itself would be decorated on the day of the wedding with fresh blossoms and all the colours of Spring flowers. Somehow, eventually, it all came together with everything being ready on time, and the day of the Equinox dawned fine and sunny.

Princess Guinevere chose to arrive at Stonehenge in the Royal Litter, even though she remembered being a prisoner within it, not so long ago. Things were different now, and she was very happy in the way that things had changed for the better. The assembled crowds gasped at the sight of her dazzling beauty as she stepped out, wearing a beautiful white wedding dress of her own design. The bride's attendants, bridesmaids – including little Rosy – and other members of the Royal party were also waiting in the sunshine to greet her and escort her inside.

King Arthur, dressed in his finest Royal robes, wearing his golden crown and carrying Excalibur, was already inside Stonehenge, where he stood upon the inlaid symbol in the centre of the great floor.

Earlier, all the foreign Royal Families who had been invited from other countries had gathered at the top of the Royal Approach. At a given signal from massed drums and horns they began to walk down the Approach in formation, then, as they turned and continued up the Processional Avenue, to everyone's amazement the Sun was seen to be directly above the building.

This Merlin had known would happen, and it had all been timed perfectly. When they reached the main entrance of Stonehenge and looked up, the Sun was exactly on the apex. A strange event was taking place; the heavens were all in alignment with the Sun.

Stonehenge appeared truly magnificent! The main doors opened, and here senior priests were on hand to welcome everyone inside, where they took their places on the seats and benches that had been specially set out for this very important occasion. Here they were joined by the Elders, members of the High Council and all the Chieftains, who entered through a different set of doors. Eventually they were all in their places, waiting expectantly for the Royal bride to arrive.

As Princess Guinevere and her attendants walked slowly into Stonehenge, a gasp of amazement and appreciation ran round the assembled congregation. Those who remembered a somewhat tomboyish girl could hardly believe their eyes as the radiantly beautiful figure walked towards them with such regal composure.

Faithful as ever, Merlin had appeared as if from nowhere as she entered, and taken her arm to escort her to the centre of the Great Hall where the King, her future husband, awaited her. Efflan was present to officiate as High Priest, and after embracing each of the Royal couple in turn, he began to perform the marriage ceremony according to ancient custom and ritual.

'A sacred union on this special day,' he called it, declaring there was no happier promise for the future than to be married on the Spring Equinox. Everything went according to plan, and as the wedding ceremony drew to a close many of the congregation were in tears, both men and women, including the normally stern-faced Reann and the rest of her companions, who had at the King's express command been allocated special seating at the back of the Great Hall, from where they had an excellent view of the ceremony.

The wedding speeches lasted several hours and time passed very quickly; few realised that during the course of the afternoon the weather had changed. It was while the ceremony was coming to an end and there was a momentary pause that the guests became aware of heavy rain beating on the roof as a sudden downpour started. It could be heard pelting down so hard that everyone fell silent and listened.

They looked up at the apex directly above them, expecting a thorough drenching, but to their amazement nothing happened! There was a sense of awe as people realised that not a single drop of rain was coming in through the hole they could see at the apex. Some even went outside the building to check that it was really raining, and returned soaked.

'How is this possible?' they all wondered. This truly was the most amazing thing that any of them had ever seen. To some, it smacked of magic, and a few suspicious glances were turned in Merlin's direction, but he continued to sit, smiling serenely, and made no comment. Many were rendered speechless by such a happening, and reacted simply by starting to clap their hands in surprise. Then, as swiftly as it had started, the rain ceased, and the guests soon forgot their fears of a soaking and returned once more, to witness this most beautiful wedding.

Afterwards, the Royal couple, now man and wife, left the building together, and returned, in procession, to the Royal Palace, accompanied by the Royal Families from overseas. The King and Queen retired to rest and change, so as to prepare themselves for the evening's festivities, while in the meantime, the others had the opportunity to enjoy any number of widely varied entertainments that had been laid on.

Later, as dusk was approaching, everyone gathered once more, outside Stonehenge. At a given signal, the main doors were opened, and Merlin appeared, to welcome them all inside. To their amazement, the centre of the Great Hall was now occupied by a huge eighteen-foot diameter Round Table, covered by a gleaming white cloth, laid with the most appetising food, and lit with large, sweet-smelling candles made of beeswax. The combination of the white cloth and candles gave it the likeness of a huge wedding cake.

As they took their seats, the guests realised that, although it was now beginning to get dark outside, the Great Hall was glowing with light – far more than the candles on the Round Table could provide.

'How could this possibly be?' they wondered, 'surely we should be in darkness, with just the flickering gleam of the table candles to give a little light?'

Sitting beside his new wife, Arthur smiled to himself. 'This is some special scheme of Merlin's,' he thought. 'But, although I'd love to know how he's achieved all this glowing light, I won't ask for once; I'll let him keep his secret. It's good not to know occasionally; we can all enjoy the wonder and spirituality of the atmosphere with open minds.'

Merlin was pleased that Arthur wanted to keep the mystery intact, and was glad that everybody was enjoying the results of his plans and calculations. As he told Efflan later, what he had done, was to have lamps placed on top of all the wooden canopies that had been built over the great seats constructed around the central open space. This had a two-fold result; the edges of the canopies, themselves, cast shadows, which fitted the Sarsen Circle, while the lamps threw their light upwards, so that the whole roof was given an atmospheric, warm golden glow.

Once over their initial surprise, the guests enjoyed a wonderful night of feasting and merrymaking. Merlin introduced the foreign monarchs to King Arthur; they had heard of the young man's bravery, and were very impressed with his kingly bearing, and modest, courteous manner. Last of all, Arthur was introduced to King Holger, of Dansk, and King Godfrey, the two most powerful men in the assembly.

Holger spoke on behalf of them both, saying: 'It is a great honour to be here! We have heard of your work to build Stonehenge, and your involvement in the defence of your country.'

'It is my privilege,' Arthur replied, 'to welcome you here today; thank you for coming.'

Holger continued, 'Our late friend, King Arthur, will be pleased, as he looks upon us from the Otherworld. We offer our hands of friendship to be a bond of lasting strength.' All three smiled and embraced each other.

Then King Godfrey said, 'We can get to know each other properly at a later date, but, for today, rejoice, and may all the blessings of the Gods go with you.'

The rest of the evening was spent in perfect harmony, and finally, as the festivities were ending, a woman began

317

to sing a joyful song in praise of marriage. On hearing this, everyone fell silent, to listen to the sound that was so beautiful and clear. The acoustics of the Great Hall were superb and everyone was convinced that there was no better place to sing than in Stonehenge!

For the next day, King Arthur, himself, had planned a surprise for everyone. He had secretly arranged, with Brad, that when the celebrations had ended, the latter would reassemble the scaffolding on the very top of the apex.

Then, the following morning, Arthur climbed up the outside of the roof and stood on the platform at the very top of Stonehenge. Arrangements had been made, that as soon as he appeared on the platform, giant horns would sound in the distance. At this signal, thousands upon thousands of people suddenly appeared on the horizon, and came running from all directions.

Seeing their King, on his lofty eminence, they approached Stonehenge; cheering, clapping, waving and shouting, at the tops of their voices. As they gathered around below him and fell silent, he drew his sword, Excalibur, and raised it high in the air, whereupon all present cheered, again, so that it sounded like a mighty roar.

He then unfurled a rope, fastened to a stout pole, and dropped the end down to Guinevere, who was standing below. She seized it and fastened it round her waist, then

Arthur pulled her up onto the platform, where she stood beside him. With her long red-gold hair blowing in the breeze, and shining brightly in the morning sunlight, Guinevere looked like the Goddess of Spring herself.

Arm in arm, the happy couple waved to everyone, again and again, while those gathered below began dancing and singing, overjoyed to see their King and Queen united together, in love and marriage.

Epilogue

It was a few months after the wedding of King Arthur and Queen Guinevere, that Merlin decided the time had come to set out on his travels, once again.

The great Centre of Excellence had been completed and was becoming established as one of the finest seats of government in the world. He, and the late King Arthur, as a result of their mutual understanding and friendship, had created one of the greatest monuments in history.

Merlin instinctively knew that now was the time to depart, and set his plans in motion. He needed to obtain additional items for the future of Stonehenge. When the time was right, he would return and disclose yet more amazing secrets. He reflected upon how the young King Arthur had proved to be an apt pupil and had learned the business of ruling his kingdom well. Merlin knew he could be left to his own devices and to rule the country with the help of Queen Guinevere, his Ministers and the High Council.

On the last day before Merlin's departure from Stonehenge, a special farewell party was held in his honour. All his friends were there, as he was, by now, universally popular. King Arthur and Queen Guinevere hosted the occasion, and everyone involved in the building of Stonehenge was invited; even Old Sniffy was included, and it was quite a surprise when he did turn up, as he'd never been known to socialise before.

'I'm only 'ere because of 'im,' he muttered gruffly, 'wouldn't do it for anyone else!'

Everyone crowded into the Great Hall and gathered round in a great circle before sitting down, many of them on the floor. Merlin stood in the centre of the circle, holding hands with Arthur and Guinevere, who were stood on either side of him.

He gazed around, and beamed a happy smile at the assembled guests. Then he spoke, saying: 'The time has come for me to leave you for a while, but I shall be taking away many memories, some that we all share. We have been through a great deal together, and I will not forget this time here with you all. You are like brothers and sisters, and I love you all dearly. Before I set out, I would like to acknowledge the remarkable courage, tenacity and determination shown by all those involved in the building of Stonehenge.

'First, I ask Reann to step forward.'

Reann stood up, and approached. As she came towards him, Merlin turned to Efflan, who handed him a Gold Badge of Honour. Merlin pinned it on Reann's robe, gripped her hand, and smiled. No one had ever seen Reann blush before, but on this occasion she did them proud, glowing 'like one of Old Sniffy's furnaces,' as Ardel murmured to his neighbour. Lost for words, but looking wonderfully serene, she resumed her seat, amid congratulations from all around her.

Then, Merlin called Brad's name, and gave him a badge also. Next was Hoel's widow, Megan, who, weeping tears of pleasure and gratitude, received hers on behalf of her late husband. Next followed Whittle, Ardel, Durrel, a very reluctant fair-haired Magnus, and last, but by no means least, Old Sniffy; as he walked up and received his badge, he too had tears in his eyes.

After the presentation, Merlin asked everyone to hug those on either side of them. As they did so, all said: 'Peace be with you!' Then Merlin, himself, was swamped with affection, as everyone tried to hug him at once.

Following the celebrations, Merlin led the guests outside Stonehenge and stood on a mighty stone, which supported one of the great buttresses. When they had gathered round him again, he made a short speech, saying, 'Some of you may have concerns that Stonehenge will deteriorate during my absences, or that it may eventually be lost, in time. This will not be so; long after all present here today are dead and gone, Stonehenge will continue to stand.

It has been built to last forever! As long as the stones remain, the power and the information, which brought Stonehenge into being, will be carried within them.' He then reached down and picked up a small baby from its mother's arms, and held the child aloft. 'Stonehenge was built for our children, and our children's children, from this time into eternity,' he continued. 'As long as there is human endeavour and human spirit, the power of the Gods will continue.' He paused, and returned the child to its mother.

'Even if the building was burnt down, and many hundreds or thousands of years were to pass, Stonehenge would not be destroyed. It is a monument that will carry a message through Time itself. One day, someone will be born who will have the ability to see and understand the truth that is carried within these stones. No matter what happens, Stonehenge will exist forever! Now I must leave you, and set out on my travels, but I promise we shall meet again, before too long. In the meantime, the Gods' blessing on you all!'

Slowly, and reluctantly, the guests departed, until only King Arthur, Queen Guinevere and Efflan remained. Merlin gathered up the few items he needed when travelling, and all three accompanied him as he walked slowly away across the High Plain.

After a while, they halted; the time for farewells had come. Efflan spoke first, saying, 'Goodbye, my friend, the Gods be with you until we meet again.' They held each other for a moment, then Efflan turned, and walked sadly back to Stonehenge.

Guinevere kissed Merlin on both cheeks, and embraced him with tears in her eyes, whispering that she would miss him more than she could say, and to come back soon.

Then she, too, left, so that Arthur and Merlin could be alone together, once more. Merlin, it was, who broke the heavy silence, remarking, 'Well, my friend! You know a great deal now - you have been a good pupil!' They laughed together.

King Arthur asked him, 'When will you return?'

Merlin replied, 'When you least expect me!'

They gave each other a final hug, then, as evening came on, Merlin walked slowly away, into the distance. Arthur stood watching him in the fading light, until he disappeared, and smiled sadly, before turning to leave.

As he reluctantly made his way back, he stopped and looked at the massive shape of Stonehenge ahead of him, majestic and serenely timeless in the gathering dusk. One by one, the stars came out to form a glittering crown above it.

'A final gesture from the Gods,' thought Arthur, 'to show that all is well. My good friend and counsellor will soon return; in his absence, we shall always remember, with eternal gratitude, that Merlin built Stonehenge!'

THE END

"There is a principle which is a bar against all information, which is proof against all arguments and which cannot fail to keep a man in everlasting ignorance - that principle is contempt prior to investigation."

HERBERT SPENCER

"The environmentally friendly puzzle that will drive you WILD!"

Even though there are a proven 19, 186 different solutions and although the Bedlam® Cube is very easy to play, it is extremely difficult to find even **one** solution.

This unique British invention has no additional packaging, being completely self contained in its own box - until you tip it out...

There are a range of colours and finishes for all ages and the wooden versions of the Bedlam® Cube are manufactured with wood from sustainable forests.

Take the ultimate challenge and tackle the hardest 3-D puzzle ever; available now from

www.bedlamcube.com